Island Weddings

CORAL ISLAND
BOOK FOUR

LILLY MIRREN

Epub ISBN: 978-1-922650-20-7

Paperback ISBN: 978-1-922650-21-4

Version 1.0

Published by Black Lab Press 2023

Lilly Mirren has asserted her right to be identified as the author of this Work in accordance with the Copyright, Designs and Patents Act 1988.

This is a work of fiction. Names, characters, organisations, places, events and incidents are either products of the author's imagination or are used fictitiously. Any resemblance to actual persons, living or dead, or actual events is purely coincidental.

Cover design by Erin D'Ameron Hill.

First published worldwide by Black Lab Press in 2023.

Brisbane, Australia.

www.blacklabpress.com

Read The Series In Order

CORAL ISLAND

The Island
The Beach Cottage
The Blue Shoal Inn
Island Weddings
The Island Bookshop
An Island Reunion

One

AS THE FERRY pulled alongside the dock, Charmaine Billings tented a hand over her eyes and studied the outline of Coral Island. She'd never visited before, but the tourist brochure she'd discovered when camping in Airlie Beach hadn't done it justice. It was stunning, surrounded by sparkling azure waters, with green hills climbing away from golden shores and quaint houses dotted here and there. It looked like something out of an advertisement for paradise. Not a real place where she might live.

"Excuse me." A man pushed past her to find his vehicle. She stepped aside with an apology, then leaned on the railing to watch as the ferry driver slowed their pace and turned the mammoth barge, making a perfect landing against the dock that would allow the parked vehicles to drive through its open mouth.

"Home sweet home," she whispered beneath her breath. She could've shouted it and still no one would've heard—the noise of the engine and the rush of the wind as it buffeted the ferry drowned out the sound of her voice.

She was moving to Coral Island.

It was crazy, of course, since she knew almost nothing about the place other than the bits and pieces she'd read. But it seemed absolutely perfect. And besides that, she had nowhere else to go. No one she was responsible for or who cared where she lay her head at night. So, why not? Why not move to a tropical island and start her life all over again?

And yet before her mother died, she'd mentioned an estranged sister who had lived on the island. She might not be there any longer, could've moved on long ago, but that vague recollection of a distant memory from a woman in and out of consciousness was her only tether to a semblance of family. And she'd come all this way in the hopes of finding her.

If her aunt was long gone, she still couldn't think of a single reason why she shouldn't move to Coral Island anyway. It was as good a place as any other. And so she'd decided to do it, even though something inside her was both flummoxed and frightened by the move.

At twenty-five years of age and with half an archaeology degree that had done absolutely nothing for her career prospects, she tried not to overthink her current situation— single, alone, with no family and no possibility of making anything more than minimum wage. If she was going to live in poverty on her own, at least she should do it somewhere picturesque. And that'd been the deciding factor for her — on paper, Coral Island appeared to be the perfect location to ignore the dumpster fire her life had become.

With all the cars now gone, she stepped out of her hiding place against the railing and walked onto firm ground. Her backpack was already heavy, and she longed to put it down, but first she had to find somewhere to stay. And given the island's identity as a tourist destination, surely that wouldn't be so difficult although she doubted there would be a back-packers' hostel, and she couldn't afford a hotel, at least not for more than a couple of nights.

She spied a bookshop. A small sign above the door announced "Eveleigh's Books". There was an old ship's wheel tacked to the wall beside the door and a rusting pelican statue perched on the weather-worn deck. It was warm, welcoming and had the kind of character that drew her attention. She loved books, so a bookshop seemed a good place for her to start. She could ask around about a place to stay and take a look at the books they had in stock at the same time.

Inside the store, she set her backpack against a wall out of the way and pushed her sweat-soaked hair back from her forehead, enjoying the feel of air-conditioning on her skin. She wandered around the store, pulling books from shelves to read the description, then returning them carefully to their place and moving on. She stopped near the mystery and thriller section for half an hour and got caught up reading one of the books she found there. When another customer squeezed by, she came rushing back to reality with embarrassing clarity and pushed the book into its place on the shelf, her cheeks warm.

The woman serving customers at the register had bright red hair in smooth curls and a laugh that was deep and melodious — every now and then, it echoed through the shop as she chatted with her customers over their purchases. When she wasn't slipping purchases into paper bags, she flitted between organising shelves and helping people find what they were looking for. Charmaine stayed out of her way. The last thing she wanted was to be kicked out of this delightful shop because she'd overstayed her welcome.

When she reached the other side of the shop, she noticed a large set of open double doors that led down three wide tiled steps. Within moments, she found herself in a quaint, warm and welcoming café. Several of the tables were occupied, but it wasn't full. Quiet music drifted through the café over the hum of low conversations.

"Would you like a table?" A middle-aged woman with

blonde hair and kind eyes peered over a set of glasses that were perched halfway down her nose. She held a menu in both hands.

Charmaine nodded, her lips pressed together. She followed the woman to a small table at the back of the café against the window and sat. The woman handed her a menu.

"My name's Beatrice, but you can call me Bea. I'll come back to take your order in a minute."

Charmaine offered her a half smile.

The woman hesitated. "Are you okay? You're a little ... pale."

"Oh, I'm fine. Pale is my normal state of being. Also, I arrived on the island an hour ago, so I don't know my way around. That, plus the heat — I'm not quite used to it yet." It felt strange to hear her own voice. She'd hardly spoken to anyone in weeks other than to say "thank you" when someone served her at the grocery shop or "excuse me" if she needed to squeeze past. Other than that, she'd kept to herself for the most part. Her voice was thin, strained, as though it could easily float away on a breath of air never to be heard again.

"Are you staying somewhere on the island or heading back this afternoon?"

Charmaine's cheeks flushed with warmth. She wasn't fond of attention. "Um... Well, I'm not sure. I haven't found anywhere to stay yet. I need a job, too. Any ideas?"

Beatrice pushed her hands into the pockets on her apron and stared out the window at the quiet street. "Oh, what a shame. I hired someone last week otherwise I would've had an opening for you. But I think I heard that Betsy Norton is hiring. If you follow that street there, you'll see her florist shop. I'm sure I can find you somewhere to stay if you give me a little while to mull it over..." She chewed on her lower lip. "Taya would probably have a place for you, but she's on the other side of the island. The resorts on this side are usually booked solid this time of year, but there's no harm in trying."

"Oh, I'm planning on living here, so I'd rather not spend all my money on a resort." Charmaine clamped her mouth shut. She didn't often share so much information with a stranger within the first five minutes of meeting them. But there was something warm and inviting about Bea that made her want to open up. She reminded Charmaine of her own mother, who'd passed away three years earlier.

Charmaine ordered a cappuccino and a slice of banana bread toasted and lathered with butter, then settled into her chair and pulled a dog-eared copy of *Persuasion* out of her pocket. She'd love to read something new, but Jane Austen's classic was still her favourite, and she'd need a library card before she could get anything else. In order to get a library card, she had to find somewhere to live first, so revisiting the beloved story was her only option for now.

Bea brought her banana bread and coffee and set them down on the table.

"Is there a library in this town?" Charmaine asked.

"There sure is. The Kellyville Library."

"Kellyville?"

Bea smiled. "That's where you are. You didn't know?"

"Oh, yes, right. Of course. I remember reading all about it."

"You read about it?"

"In a brochure on Coral Island."

"Do you have family here? Or friends?"

Charmaine shook her head. She wasn't ready to talk about the aunt who might possibly live here, whose name she didn't recall and who she hadn't seen since she was an infant. The revelation would only lead to more questions. "It looked like a nice place ... in the brochure."

"Bit of an adventurer then, are you?" Bea tidied some empty cups from the next table.

"Something like that."

"Well, let me know if you need anything else. And welcome to the Island."

* * *

After she'd finished her coffee and banana bread, Charmaine collected her backpack and set off to find the florist shop Bea had mentioned. The town was like something out of a post-card. The main street had quaint, old-fashioned shops up and down both sides. The streets were clean, with greenery and trees dotted here and there in well-maintained garden beds. Shoppers wandered along the pavement or darted into and out of the retail outlets.

It didn't take her long to locate *Betsy's Florals*. There was a huge picture window that displayed vases full of colourful flowers. Artwork hung on the walls. The narrow shop was painted a bright white with blue trim. When she pushed through the heavy timber door, a bell rang above her head.

"Can I help you?" a tremulous voice called from the back.

Soon an elderly woman appeared, her eyebrows raised in question. She had grey curls and sparkling blue eyes and wore a black apron over a silk kaftan in swirls of blue and green.

"Hi, I was told you might be hiring. My name's Char-maine, and I'm new to the island. I'm looking for work."

The woman held out her hand with a broad smile. "Plea-sure to meet you, honey. I'm Betsy, and I'm looking for someone to help me out here in the store. You have any retail experience?"

Betsy's American accent was subtle enough that Char-maine figured she'd lived in Australia for a long time. She wondered what had brought Betsy to a place like Coral Island — so remote, tucked away from the rest of the world.

"Yes, I worked in a dress shop back home."

"I'm desperate, and that's a fact. If you can start tomorrow, you have the job. I'll need some details, of course, and I'll try to find an application form to give you. I've got one lying around here somewhere. Now, where did I put that thing?" Betsy shuffled some papers next to the cash register, then bent over to look through drawers beneath it.

"Thanks for this. I really appreciate it," Charmaine said.

Betsy straightened with a grunt. "You're so welcome, honey. You're doing me a favour, I promise you that. Where are you staying?" She eyed Charmaine's backpack.

"I don't know yet. I'm going to find somewhere just as soon as I leave here. I figured getting a job was my first priority. Maybe someone will let me rent from them now that I'm employed..."

Betsy's eyes narrowed. "Well, if you're interested, there's a small apartment upstairs. You go up those back steps, and it sits right above where we're standing now. It's nothing special, but it's comfortable enough. If you're willing to open and close the shop each day for me, keep an eye on things when I'm not around, I'll let you stay free of charge. I've been hoping to have someone take the load off me now that I'm spending more time caring for my granddaughter. Of course, I'll need to speak to your past employer first."

"Wow, that would be amazing. Thank you!" It seemed more than luck had brought her to the florist shop. A job and a place to stay—it was overwhelming. It'd been so long since anyone had done something kind for her. She fought to keep the tears at bay.

"Do you go by Charmaine or Char?" Betsy asked.

"People usually call me Chaz."

"Very Aussie," Betsy replied with a grin. "Chaz it is." She

handed Charmaine a sheaf of papers. "There you go—the application form. Here's a pen. You can sit over there by the window and fill it out. Then I'll show you the apartment upstairs, and you can move your things into it. Do you have anything else with you?"

"No, this is all of it," Charmaine replied, patting the backpack with one hand over her shoulder.

Betsy grunted. "Fine, traveling light is the best way to go. I used to travel light. But that was a long time ago. Write down your references here, and I'll give them a call. I thank my lucky stars that you walked in here today, I was beginning to wonder if I'd ever find someone to help me manage this place. It's a lot at my age. You've really made my day."

Two

THE CAFE, *Bea's Coffee*, buzzed with a large crowd of tourists the next day. A large segment of the group seemed to be a birthday party for a group of six-year-olds. The noise level had risen exponentially since they arrived, and one of her staff was busy cleaning spilled chocolate milk off the floor, balloons bobbing around her.

Beatrice Rushton was too busy to notice when the strange girl from the day before wandered in and found a table. But by the time the crowd had begun to shift through the front door and headed for the dock where the ferry was already churning and chugging itself into place to be boarded, she spied the girl seated at the same table as she'd occupied on her previous visit.

Bea studied her carefully as she wiped down the espresso machine. There was something so interesting about her. It was as though she was a small, injured bird in need of mothering, and an inner voice in Bea's head pushed her to take her under her wing. She was pale and freckled, with long, wispy light brown hair that she'd pulled into a messy ponytail. Her large grey eyes were fixed on her phone screen. Her small lips were pursed, and she was busy tapping away at something.

She was thin and angular, and held herself in a way that made it seem as though she must always be uncomfortable. What was her name again? Charmaine, or something like that. Bea was usually good with names, but these days, there were so many of them — people who came and went from her life on a minute-by-minute basis.

She scanned the café, noticing that Janice, one of the bookshop staff, had stepped through their adjoining door and leaned against the wall to chat with one of Bea's waiters, a handsome, if somewhat thin, teenaged boy with braces. She'd hired a couple of local high school boys to help out during the holidays, and it'd been such a distraction to Evie's staff that they'd held a meeting about it to discuss what on earth to do.

Neither one of them were keen on the idea of admonishing their employees over what was undoubtedly a miasma of hormones swirling around their young bodies. In fact, Bea could vaguely remember the feeling herself. But there was work to be done, and she didn't have the energy or the desire to do it all on her own.

Thankfully, at that moment, the boy noticed her watching and said his goodbyes, hurrying to clear a table. She was grateful she hadn't needed to say anything to him. Other than, "Hey, could you stop flirting and clear a table?" she wasn't exactly sure how to phrase her request. And the words, even in her head, sounded harsh and made her feel extremely old. When had she stepped over the line from flirter to admonisher?

She couldn't pinpoint the moment when her youthfulness had vanished, but it'd probably been somewhere around the time her husband left her with a newborn baby to go on an extended business trip. She'd ended up seated on the floor at midnight in a puddle of tears with dirty nappies piled up beside her, a wailing infant in her arms and an intense dawning realisation that life would never be the same again.

Her entire world had changed in a flash. One moment she'd been a fun, flirty, university student. The next, she was a college dropout, married mother with dark bags beneath her eyes from lack of sleep. She'd realised that her life no longer revolved around herself and her new, handsome and charismatic husband, but around this squalling, fist-pumping, red-faced creature that never slept for long and couldn't seem get enough milk to drink no matter how long she fed for. That had been twenty years ago. Life since then had certainly flown by. There was nothing like raising children to turn passing time into a pinwheel on a windy day.

She was jolted back to the present by the sound of a balloon bursting. A bevy of children scooted out the café door and into the brilliant sunshine ahead of a harried mother. Bea finished up with the espresso machine, then wiped her hands dry. The girls were coming to see her, and she was very much looking forward to it.

"The girls," as she called them, were her lifelong friends from her school years. When her twenty-five-year marriage came to an end the three women had been her saving grace. Along with her father and brother, who had welcomed her back into their lives even though she'd spent years avoiding them and Coral Island.

Evie owned the bookshop next door and was the first to arrive. She shucked off a long black apron and waved to Bea as she marched through the café. "I'm exhausted! That was a big group. I've never seen so many readers in one place before. Dying for a coffee!"

"Coffee coming up. Any preference for cake?"

"Do you have mud cake? It's one of those days. I think I'm hormonal." She kissed Bea on the cheek across the counter, then spun on her heel to find a table.

Taya was next to arrive. She swanned in, her hair perfectly coiffed, a dark sleek bob that brushed her thin shoulders. She tugged a pair of designer sunglasses from her face and peered around the café until her gaze landed on Bea. Then she smiled widely, her red lips parting to reveal a set of straight white teeth.

"Darling, you look wonderful!" Beatrice squealed and rushed to hug her friend. "You're back!"

"You knew I was coming," Taya replied, wrapping her arms around Bea, then taking a step back to smile down at her. She was much taller than Beatrice and always gave the impression she'd had a glam team at her disposal to make her up before every event.

"You said you were, but I wasn't sure I should believe you."

"It was only a business trip. I'll be doing a lot more of them from now on since I'm working with Dad. Or *for* Dad, really. He says I should think of us as partners, but he's the boss. He wants me to get to know the business from top to bottom. So, even though I'm only assistant manager at our local Paradise Resort, he's taking me under his wing because he says I'll inherit the whole company one day and he wants me to know everything about it first."

"It makes sense. You're perfect for the job," Bea replied. "Grab a seat. Evie's found us a table in the back. I'll be there in a minute with coffee and cake. I want to hear about *everything*."

"Time to party!" Penny burst through the front door with arms raised high.

Bea laughed. "You almost gave me a heart attack."

"You must be on edge. Perhaps you should slow down a little. We don't want you getting burned out." Penny hurried to give her a kiss on the cheek. "Sorry I'm late. I had an emergency with a bilby that was hit by a car. Poor little thing. It had a broken leg, but I think we'll be able to save it. Did I miss anything?"

"Only a big group of tourists, including a dozen children plus balloons."

Penny grimaced. "Glad I was late now." She laughed as she made her way to greet Taya and Evie. "Just kidding. I love kids. And balloons."

Beatrice put together a tray of coffees and slices of cake on plates, then carried it to the table and set everything up between the friends. Then she slumped into a chair with a sigh.

"It feels good to get off my feet. Wow, that was crazy."

"Amen to that," Evie agreed, reaching for her cake. "Now, Taya, you've got to tell us all about what's going on with you and the new man."

Taya's cheeks reddened. "You mean Andrew."

"Yes," Bea said. with a wink. "Come on—spill the tea."

Taya pressed her lips together, then smiled. "We've decided to try dating."

Bea squealed. Evie clapped her hands together.

Penny laughed. "I never thought I'd see the day, Taya Eldridge."

Taya grunted. "Honestly, neither did I. But we met for lunch last week, and we agreed that we have a special connection and we're both mature enough to keep our work relationship professional while dating. At least, I hope we are." She sipped her coffee. "So, what do you think? Is it crazy to date my boss?"

"It's not crazy at all," Bea said. "It's wonderful. You've been single for so long and now you're finally in a good place professionally and romantically. New opportunities, new adventures... it suits you."

"You're glowing," Evie said.

Penny's eyes glistened. "I'm really happy for you, sweetie."

"It's a trial run, nothing serious. I'll be focusing a lot on my career. and he's very busy with work as well. Neither one of us wants to dive into anything too deep right now. But we went out for dinner on Friday night and I have to admit, it was absolutely delightful. I haven't enjoyed myself so much in a very long time. We talked for hours, laughed more than I thought possible, and had so much in common."

"You're both so glamorous. Evie and I saw him from a distance when we were at the resort the other day for a facial," Bea said. "You suit each other."

"And so tall," Evie added.

Taya laughed, pushing her hair back from her face with long, manicured fingers. "I'm not tall. You're just a bunch of shorties."

"I prefer vertically challenged," Bea pouted.

"Gravitationally sensitive?" Evie asked, a finger pressed to her lips.

"Perfect," Bea agreed.

Taya shook her head. "However you want to term it, I happen to agree that we suit one another. But I would never have thought so when I first met him. I thought he was a slick, sleazy businessman who only cared about profit margins and couldn't see the beauty in my inn. But I couldn't have been more wrong about him. He's compassionate, caring, creative and highly aware of every aspect of the business. He's been so careful to include me in every decision about the direction we're taking the inn."

"I think the inn looks amazing," Evie said as she sliced off a piece of cake with her fork. "You've both done a fantastic job with it."

"It's in very good hands, so I've been perfectly relaxed. Even if they're making changes that I would've grimaced over previously. Well, almost relaxed... I do occasionally experience pangs of anxiety. I get over it fairly quickly when I remember that it's no longer my responsibility and I don't have to be there at five a.m. the next day to open the doors and get the bread into the oven because the chef called in sick."

"You seem happy, so I'm happy," Penny said.

"How's the wedding planning coming?" Taya asked as she sipped her cappuccino delicately.

Penny shrugged. "Fine, I guess."

"What does that mean?" Bea asked.

"It means I'm ignoring the wedding plans beautifully," Penny replied.

Evie laughed. "Oh, sweetie, you've got to actually plan it, or it won't happen."

"I know," Penny replied with a groan. "But I'm so busy with the refuge at the moment. The grant we got from the government has been fantastic—we can afford to keep the lights on. The problem is, now we're expected to do a lot more. We have people calling us from all over the place with animals to take in. I'm loving it, of course. But I don't know how to manage it all. I've got so much paperwork to do and not enough hands..." She held her hands up, waved them around as if to show off there were only two of them.

"I can help," Bea offered.

"Thanks," Penny replied. "But you have your own business to run, and I need to make some decisions before anyone can really step in. Plus, Rowan keeps taking jobs overseas, so he's gone all the time and I miss him. I don't know how this is going to work — we're both too busy to get married."

"Is he going to keep his job as a journalist?" Taya asked. "Because Coral Island isn't exactly a hub for international travel. It takes ages to get to an airport on the mainland, let alone to a city where you can fly internationally."

"I don't know what he's going to do. We need to sit down and have a serious conversation about a few things ... and soon. It's frustrating with us both working so much. We hardly have time for a romantic date night, so when we do see each other, we don't want to spoil the time together talking about serious things. Of course, we'll have to, since we're getting married and there are things we need to figure out."

"Trust me, it's better to talk about the big issues before you're married rather than after," Beatrice said. She wished she and her ex had spoken openly before they were married. It might've discouraged her from going forward with the wedding if she'd known more about him and his perspective, although she doubted it.

She'd been determined to find someone to settle down with after the love of her life had broken her heart. She'd recently lost her mother and was so overcome with grief, Aidan hadn't known how to help her and instead had accepted an offer to play professional football in Brisbane.

There wasn't likely to be anything that would've stopped her jumping into her marriage with complete abandon the way she did after all that heartbreak. It was as though she was drowning, and Preston was a life preserver. She could ignore the pain in her heart and instead focus on him and becoming his wife. It'd been the perfect excuse to push her family away as well, since seeing them only reminded her of what she'd lost.

Bea noticed that the young woman, Charmaine, seemed to be listening in on their conversation. She was seated at the next table and held a dog-eared book in her hands, but her face was slanted in their direction.

"Charmaine? Is that right?" Bea addressed her.

The girl looked up, cheeks flushing red. "Uh, yeah, that's it."

"I remember you from yesterday. How did you go at Betsy's?"

The girl smiled. "She gave me a job and a place to stay. I'm living above the shop in a little flat."

"Wow, that's fantastic," Bea replied. "These are my friends, Evie, Taya and Penny."

"Nice to meet you," Charmaine said, waving to the group.

"Charmaine has moved here from..." Bea's eyes narrowed. She couldn't recall if the girl had told her where she'd come from, but she was curious to know.

"All around... I move a lot," Charmaine replied.

"That's interesting." Penny laughed. "I never move. I've lived in the same house most of my life. I'll probably die there."

"Wow," Charmaine responded, eyes wide. "I can't imagine doing that."

"Boring is probably the best way to describe it."

"No, I wouldn't say that. I'd love to have that kind of stability. I don't have anywhere that's home. Not really."

"Well, maybe Coral Island will be that for you," Taya suggested.

"I hope so."

"Penny's getting married soon," Bea said. "That's a big enough change for now, I'd say."

"Congratulations. I couldn't help overhearing that you're having trouble planning it. I've done some wedding planning in the past. If you need help, I'm looking for extra work so I can save up to buy myself a bike. I'd be happy to help."

"Really?" Penny's eyebrows arched high. "A wedding planner on Coral Island? I never thought I'd see the day. But honestly, that would be such a big help. You're sure you have the time to do it?"

Charmaine nodded. "Absolutely. We can meet to talk about the kinds of things you're looking for, and I'll put together some ideas to show you."

Bea listened as Penny and Charmaine continued chatting about the wedding before Charmaine excused herself and left the café. It would've been wise for Penny to ask for references or dig into the girl's background a little bit before hiring her, but she wasn't about to interfere. If Penny was happy to do business that way, who was Beatrice to tell her otherwise?

Penny had always been a free spirit whose choices in life were often impulsive and who responded to things with a raw emotion that Bea rarely displayed. Sometimes she wished she could be as passionate as Penny, but at the same time, she didn't want the drama it often brought. She'd experienced more than enough drama for her taste in recent years, and she certainly didn't need more of it.

* * *

After Taya and Penny had left, Evie helped Bea washed the last of the cups and plates. The café was empty. The afternoon rush was over, and Bea was looking forward to closing the cafe and heading home to Fudge, her sweet little pug, and hopefully a quiet night with her boyfriend, Aidan. Just then, Aidan walked into the café and strode across the hardwood floor to plant a kiss on her lips. His warm arms wrapped her up, and he held her close to his firm chest. She was so grateful the two of them had found each other again after so many years apart.

"Are you almost finished here?"

She smiled at him. "Very close. Be done in a minute."

"What can I do to help?"

"You can put the chairs on the tables, if you like."

He got to work, and Beatrice set about compiling a list of supplies to order while the rest of the staff swept and mopped. She was finally at a place in her life where everything was going smoothly. Harry had recovered from Lyme disease six months earlier and was now in perfect health once again. He was back at university, enjoying his studies, and on his way to becoming a doctor.

Her daughter, Danita, was loving her interior design degree program and had even helped a local business in Sydney redesign their fit-out for a small fee. She was on her way to becoming a competent professional, and Beatrice couldn't be prouder of both her adult children. They were sensible and rational, made good choices, worked hard, were responsible, and seemed to be tackling life in Sydney with verve. And both had accepted their parents' recent divorce with aplomb.

The icing on the cake was that Bea and her father had reconciled after a strained relationship over many years. She'd avoided Coral Island, and him by extension, since visiting it had conjured up painful memories of the mother she'd lost at a tender age. He'd had some health issues recently as well, reminding her that he wouldn't be around forever.

She intended to take every opportunity from now on to rebuild the family she'd pushed away all those years ago. And hopefully give her own children an example of how important those relationships were to her, and how family could fight, spend time apart and have disagreements, but at the end of the day, they were inextricably connected. Family was more important to her at this stage of her life than it had ever been. She only wondered why she'd taken so long to figure out what many people seemed to understand implicitly.

Life was good.

The fact that she was enjoying it back home on Coral Island was something she'd never thought she'd get a chance to experience after more than two decades in the city. But it was her home once again, and the beauty and tranquillity of life on the tropical island wasn't something she'd ever take for granted again.

As she finished making up the café's shopping list, her phone rang. She slipped it out of her apron pocket and held it to her ear.

"Hello?"

"Hi, Mum."

"Dani, it's so lovely to hear your voice. I was just thinking about you."

"You were? Good things, I hope."

"I'm so proud of how well you're doing. It makes me happy to know that you're enjoying your studies and your life, even if I don't get to see you every day."

"Thanks, Mum. That means a lot to me. In fact, I have news. That's why I'm calling."

"Lovely—I'm glad you thought to include me. What's going on, sweetheart?"

There was a pause.

"I've met someone."

Bea's heart skipped a beat. "You've met someone? That's great, honey."

Even if change sometimes made her nervous, she reminded herself that this was a *good* thing. Love was something she longed for both of her children to find, and when they did, she'd be kind, supportive and completely on board. She trusted them to be sensible in the people they ultimately chose to spend their lives with.

Dani had always been fussy — she'd been a picky eater as a toddler and had rarely found any hobbies she'd considered worth pursuing. When she did commit to something, she always did so with every part of her being. She called it "hyper focus," but Bea saw it as a strength — her daughter could achieve anything she put her mind to because she put every ounce of herself into it.

She'd been told it came along with the autism Dani was diagnosed with several years earlier. So, when she finally did fall in love, Bea imagined she'd be choosy about the man she gave her heart to, and that she'd likely give him her all. Bea only hoped he'd deserve it. "What's his name?"

"Damien Lachey. I met him in my architecture class. I told

you about him, I think. He's wonderful and kind. You're going to love him."

"I didn't know you were taking an architecture class. And I didn't know you were seeing him. You said he was a friend."

"We're more than friends now, much more. And I signed up this semester. I thought it'd help with my design aesthetic. Anyway, he's amazing, and I've fallen in love with the class as well. I'm thinking of switching over to architecture next year."

Bea frowned. *Love?* Already? What happened to being picky?

Another adjustment to her degree program at this stage seemed irresponsible. She'd already taken a year off social work before changing to interior design. At this rate, her daughter would never get a qualification. "Changing again? Is that a good idea, honey? You'll have completed almost two years of your design course by then. Shouldn't you finish it first and then think about doing something else?"

"You don't understand, Mum. Damien says it's the best way to make use of my talent. That I'm wasted on interior design. He sees a lot of potential in me. Besides, I'll be able to transfer some credits."

"Damien sounds like he has a lot of opinions for a twenty-year-old kid," Bea snapped. She stopped herself and squeezed her mouth shut. She couldn't help it sometimes—it was hard to let go of parenting her children like they were still ... well, children. But Dani was an adult and responsible for her own decisions. Bea was paying for her daughter's education, along with their father, so surely the two of them should get input into the decisions she made.

"Twenty-year-olds aren't kids, Mum," Dani huffed. "And anyway, Damien isn't twenty. He's thirty-six."

Bea's adrenaline spiked. "What? Why is a thirty-six-year-old man studying first-year architecture and getting into romances with twenty-one-year-old girls?"

21

"Mum, you're being unreasonable. I'm not a girl—I'm a woman. And he's not studying first-year—he's teaching it. He's the lecturer. He lives in this amazing flat with no furniture—it's all just cushions on the floor. Can you believe it?"

Bea couldn't believe it. She also couldn't believe her daughter was calling a flat without furniture *amazing,* but instead of saying so outright, she murmured something indecipherable in response.

"He wears beautifully coloured tunics instead of the formal shirt and pants that most of the lecturers wear. And he smokes this funny-looking thing with a long hose... I don't know what it is, but he's really into different cultures and says we have to open our minds to things beyond our own understanding. That we can't limit ourselves to the things we know."

Bea continued the conversation with Dani, but couldn't focus on anything other than her daughter's revelation. A stone formed in the pit of Bea's gut. She felt like she'd be sick at any moment. They'd held Dani's twenty-first birthday party in Sydney several months earlier. It'd been the first time Bea had seen her ex-husband Preston since he'd begun dating her former friend, Annie. She'd been nervous to bump into the two of them again now that they were an established couple, but in the end, she'd managed to stay out of their way for most of the night.

But her most vibrant memory from the event was her sweet young daughter on the dance floor, surrounded by other laughing, squealing young women. It'd struck Bea then how quickly the time had passed. She recalled in a flash the newborn baby riding home in the impossibly large car seat, with Bea and Preston anxiously driving through the Sydney traffic in pelting rain. The toddler who threw tantrums and food, but who had the sweetest smile in the world and loved to draw. The girl who begged to go to the beach on weekends so she could build sandcastles and ride her boogie board on the small waves close to the shore. She'd brought so much joy into their lives — both her and Preston. It was hard to believe she was twenty-one years old and halfway through a degree.

Dani had enjoyed the celebration — had invited all her old high school friends as well as her new university ones. There'd been an eclectic mix of people at the venue, but Bea didn't recall a thirty-six-year-old man in a brightly coloured tunic. She was certain she wouldn't have forgotten someone who fit that description. Dani had seemed so young to be turning twenty-one and Bea wasn't quite ready to see her as an adult. But she'd been married by Dani's age, something she had to constantly remind herself of whenever she was tempted to treat Danita like a child.

She grimaced, pressing a hand to her forehead as Dani continued raving about the new man in her life. Bea stumbled to a chair and lowered herself into it, then told her daughter goodbye in the most chipper, sing-song voice she could muster and hung up the phone. Her head fell into her hands, and she stared at the tabletop.

This couldn't be happening. Her beautiful twenty-one-year-old daughter was in love with a thirty-six-year-old professor who was clearly taking advantage of his position to influence her. She'd raised her daughter better than that.

Dani knew all about female oppression—Bea had made sure of it. She'd given her lectures about predators and taking care of herself, looking out for people who might take advantage, not making life decisions based on a boyfriend. If only she'd had someone tell her the same when she was young, her life might've turned out very differently. Sometimes she felt as though she'd harped on about it far too often and that her children might never trust anyone in their entire lives.

And now this.

It wasn't likely this man was serious about Dani. She'd

never witnessed a relationship between a professor and a student personally. All she knew was that a thirty-six-year-old man was making her daughter fall in love with him and encouraging her to adopt major changes in her life. Beatrice was no longer her main influencer, and she felt completely out of control and as though she might hyperventilate at any moment.

"One last table to go." Aidan stopped beside her, waiting. "Are you okay?"

She shook her head. "Dani called. She's met a thirty-six-year-old professor who smokes drugs and lives on cushions. They're dating, and now she wants to switch her studies to an architecture major."

Aidan's eyes widened. "That's a lot to take in. But perhaps you shouldn't get too worked up over it. Don't you remember being twenty-one? We all had at least one crazy relationship and did things we're not proud of, thinking back. At least, I know I did."

She regarded at him with horror. "I had a terrible crush on a narcissistic jerk... and by twenty-one, I was married to him."

"Good point." He sat beside her and took her hand in his. "You're upset over someone you don't know a lot about. I'm sure it's not as bad as it seems in your head right now. Dani's a sensible girl. She'll come around."

"I'm her mother..." She almost choked on the words.

"I know you are. And you're a wonderful mother. But she's an adult, and she has to make her own choices."

"I never thought letting go would be so hard."

"Let's sleep on it, and you can talk to her tomorrow. I'm sure everything will be okay."

Three

OPENING the shop was easy enough for Charmaine. In fact, she'd already fallen in love with the picturesque shop and the cramped, narrow apartment above it. She popped the last bite of toast into her mouth and chewed as she tied on her shoes. Then she pulled a hat onto her head and trotted down the winding staircase. The building was old, the walls newly painted. Her footsteps echoed on the timber stairs. She pushed open the door that led into the shop, then went to the front to unlock the main entrance.

The street outside was mostly empty apart from several clusters of schoolchildren walking together to the nearby state school. They giggled and chatted, their high-pitched voices ringing out through the still, cool morning air. She moved about the shop setting up clean vases ready for flowers to be added, sweeping the floor clear of any leaves that'd fallen the previous day, and dusting the already clean ledges that held their most popular arrangements.

She loved the community feel of this place. It was so different to the city. Everyone seemed to know and care about each other. There were hardly any cars at this time of morning, with most of the locals preferring to walk or ride their bikes to get around town. That suited her fine. She'd never gotten her driver's license since in the city, she could manage using buses and trains. One day, she'd have to take the time to get her license, but for now, a bike would be the perfect solution to her transportation problem.

As soon as Betsy arrived at the shop, Charmaine asked if she could take a walk, and Betsy said it was fine since they had nothing much to do until later in the morning when there were several appointments booked. Charmaine tied her hair in a ponytail and looped it through the back of her cap. Then she stepped outside into the bright sunshine. Her treasured easel and paints were tucked safely into a bag upstairs and she'd brought her camera with her to capture still-frames of life on the island. She loved creating art. It was her one true passion in life.

She tried to get out and about whenever she was in a new place and take photos — it gave her a chance to get to know the area in a way she usually wouldn't. She spent most of her life walking with her head down trying to avoid eye contact with strangers, ignoring the lives going on around her. But with a camera in her hands, she faced everything head-on, looking for the best shot, finding ways to open herself up to the world. Then she could take the photos back to her flat, set up her easel and paint. The hours would pass in a flash — she never kept track of time when she was creating.

There was a turtle swimming by when she sat down on the dock. She snapped a few images as best she could, of its shell as it surfaced, its head popping up and then disappearing once again into the clear blue waters of the Coral Sea. Next, she found a patch of yellow wildflowers on the dunes, followed by some particularly colourful shells. There were several children playing at the water's edge, digging up pippies with their toes when the water receded, then splashing each other in fits of giggles. She took photographs of it all.

When she returned to the flower shop, she saw that Betsy had company.

There was a man with a small girl, maybe ten years old, standing close to Betsy by the counter. He was shouting and waving his arms around. Charmaine paused with her hand on the doorknob, unsure if she should go in and rescue her boss or if the exchange was private and she should leave. In the end, her concern for Betsy's safety pushed her forwards, her stomach tying itself into knots the moment she opened the door and the sound of his raised voice hit her like a slap to the face.

"Too many lies. It's enough already. You have to tell the truth."

The man spun about as she entered. He glared at her, then stalked from the shop, leaving the girl behind. Betsy's face was red. She inhaled a slow breath as Charmaine approached.

"Are you all right?" Charmaine asked.

Betsy pushed a smile across her face. "I'm fine. This is my granddaughter, Samantha. She comes to visit me most mornings before school so I can walk with her. She'll be back this afternoon to do her homework in the shop with us. Won't you, honey?"

Sam offered her a wobbly grin. Her eyes were wet. "Yep. Hi."

Charmaine crouched down in front of her. "Hi, Samantha. It's so nice to meet you. I'm Chaz. Do you mind if I call you Sam? I'll be here when you finish school. I'd love to see what you're working on."

The girl's face brightened. "You can call me Sam, I don't mind." She set her backpack on the floor and began digging through it. "I've done all my homework for today."

She pulled out a booklet and flicked through the pages, showing off her work.

"That's great! Well done," Charmaine told her. Then the girl disappeared into the back room.

"She loves it in there. It's her own little hideaway," Betsy said with a smile.

Sam emerged again with a hairbrush and hair bands, then knelt in front of Betsy.

"I meant to tell you, Betsy. I ran into someone named Penny St James at the café on the corner. Do you know her?"

"Yes, I know Penny." Betsy combed Sam's hair and began plaiting it in two long braids.

"I offered to help plan her wedding. She's going to pay me to do it. Do you mind?"

"That's fine. As long as you do it on your own time."

"Thanks, I will definitely do that. And she's going to order flowers from us as well."

"That's wonderful — it'll be a lovely wedding, I'm sure. We have to get to school now. Thank you, Chaz. I'll be back in a few minutes." Betsy led the girl out the front door. Sam's uniform was neatly ironed, and her hair hung in two long, brown plaits on either side of her head. Her backpack was enormous, and she was so small carrying it through the door as the bell dinged overhead.

Charmaine watched them go, wondering what the shouting had been about. Adrenaline still coursed through her veins from the anxiety the man's voice and demeanour had produced in her. Charmaine didn't like conflict. She particularly hated yelling.

Betsy was so well dressed and had wonderful manners, and she was always perfectly groomed and wore expensive silk kaftans every day. The man she'd said was her son wore old, soiled work clothes and had an unkempt beard and wild brown hair streaked with grey. His stomach protruded over the waistband of his shorts, and he'd appeared completely out of control. He was so unlike Betsy in every possible way, it was hard for Charmaine to believe he was her son. Why would he be shouting at his own mother? And what were the lies she'd told?

She tucked her camera away behind the register and got to work. Painting would have to wait until after her shift was over. Already she was running through the colours, brushes and mediums she'd use for each piece in her head. It helped her process her feelings, to tune out the noise of the world and to calm her nerves. When she was painting, or sculpting, sketching or colouring, she could forget her troubles and focus on the act of creation.

Until then, she had orders to fill and flowers to arrange. She'd already learned so much from Betsy and it'd become another form of meditative creation for her. Pulling flowers from each of the pots and bringing them together to make a beautiful work of art, the day would pass by quickly. She only wondered if the conflict with Betsy's son would be an ongoing issue.

Four

POINT PROSPECT WAS sunny when they arrived for the engagement party. Penny drove there in her car while Rowan rode with Brad in his yacht. He'd agreed to bring it to the point for the day so they could all swim and picnic and enjoy the view from the vantage of the ocean.

It was a beautiful day, as long as the rain clouds stayed on the horizon and didn't drift too close. Penny was excited and a little nervous about all their loved ones coming together to celebrate. She hadn't seen her parents in person in six months and wasn't sure how they'd go sharing space with Rowan's family.

Since June Clements last saw Penny's parents, her ex-husband, Buck, had gone to prison for murdering Penny's grandmother. Now he was behind bars, awaiting trial as the police built their case against him. She wasn't sure how much evidence they had, but she hoped it would put him away for the rest of his life. The fact that she'd recently discovered he was her biological father only further complicated the matter.

Her mother had been sixteen when she fell pregnant with Penny. Buck had been an adult and had taken advantage of his friends' daughter. How on earth would the two families manage to co-exist peacefully, given their history? Even thinking about it made her heart hurt and her gut churn.

There were so many connections crisscrossing between the guests coming to their party that she wasn't sure she could keep them all straight. The plan was to stop any conflict before it might happen by separating the guests who had a grievance against one another. But at this point, that seemed impossible.

"Are you okay?" Beatrice asked as she opened a folding table on the grass and pegged a tablecloth in place so it wouldn't be blown away by an unexpected gust of wind.

"I don't know." Penny chewed a fingernail. "Mum and Dad should stay away from June ... but then Betsy's coming too. Should I keep them apart? Because Buck is Betsy's brother, and she was his alibi. Then there's my brother Rob, who's angry with Mum for not telling me Buck is my father. They haven't spoken in weeks. I'm not sure how to keep the peace. Honestly, my head is pounding and I want to throw up, and no one's even arrived yet."

Beatrice shook her head and reached out a hand to pat Penny's arm. "Sounds to me like you're just going to have to buckle up for the ride. You can't keep them all apart. If it goes badly, it goes badly. Fretting over it will only ruin the entire day for you. Let them shout at each other if they want to. Heck, they can even throw potato salad." She set a bowl of potato salad on the table with a flourish. "But you and Rowan shouldn't let it get to you. Today is all about the two of you and your love for one another. A love that crosses the barriers and defies the odds. You're getting married! After all this time! That's worth celebrating. If there's a food fight—well, maybe you should simply join in and have fun with it."

Penny laughed, the tension along her shoulders easing slightly. "You're right. This is silly. I can't control them any more than I can control that storm headed our way."

Beatrice set a bowl of coleslaw beside the potatoes with a shrug. "It's hard to let go when we care so much."

"I haven't had enough time to think it through, either, since I've been so busy with work. But Rowan has been great —when he's at home. He's really taken a lot of the load around the house. He even fixed my car the other day."

"That's great," Bea said. "I had no idea he was so handy."

"Me either. The problem is, he's hardly ever home. When he has an assignment, he's gone for weeks at a time."

"Do you think you can keep going like that?"

"Not long term. But I don't want him to give up his career for me."

"Isn't that what *he* wants?"

Penny sighed. "He says he longs to stay on the island and have a simpler life, but I know him. If he doesn't have an occupation, he'll go mad."

Bea shrugged. "Or maybe he'll settle down and the two of you will be deliriously happy together."

"I like the sound of that." Penny grinned.

* * *

When Penny's parents arrived at the party, she kissed their cheeks and found them seats far away from Betsy Norton, June Clements and the rest of Rowan's family.

"You look thin, love," Mum said, with a worried crease across her forehead. Her wispy grey hair blew wildly in the breeze that blew in off the ocean.

"I'm happy. And far too busy to eat."

Her mother offered a wan smile. "As long as you're okay."

"I'm great. Here, would you like some potato salad?"

Penny was quickly occupied with feeding people and chatting to friends and family as they arrived at the party. The first

33

she knew of any conflict was the sound of raised voices from the picnic shelter by the barbecue.

She glanced over her shoulder to see Rowan standing with BBQ tongs in one hand, a worried expression on his face, as he watched his mother argue with Penny's mother. She could tell he was debating whether to get involved or let them go at it.

Penny hurried to intervene, nerves churning in her gut.

"You've got a lot of nerve saying something like that to me," June Clements hissed.

Ruby St. James scowled. "You were in on the whole thing. I know you were."

"I don't know what you're talking about. Clearly you've lost your mind. But what's new?" June pressed her hands to her wide hips. "You can't blame me for something like that."

"You married him while I was pregnant. You had to know what he'd done and what he was up to."

"I had no idea! I told you that at the time." June threw her hands up in the air. "It's like speaking to a wall."

"At least I'm not a hussy!"

"Ladies, come on now. Let's put the past behind us. This is a celebration," Penny begged.

Ruby smiled at Penny. "Of course, honey. That's exactly what I wanted to do before June accosted me."

"Accosted you? I'll show you what accosting looks like..." She lunged at Ruby who scuttled backwards and tripped. She fell and rolled onto her back with a cry of pain.

Rowan quickly bundled his mother down to the beach, one arm around her shoulders as he whispered angrily at her.

Penny's stepfather, Henry St James, stooped to crouch by Ruby's side. "Are you okay, honey?"

She sat up, one hand clutching at her back. "Ouch."

Betsy rushed forward and helped Henry bring Ruby to her feet. Ruby grimaced, then glared at Betsy. "I'm fine, thank you."

Betsy raised both hands as if in surrender. "Only trying to help, honey."

"I think you've helped enough!" Ruby said, her eyes glistening with unshed tears. "More than enough."

"I'd love to know what you mean by that," Betsy stated, taking a step back, her face clouding.

"You know exactly what I mean — your brother murdered my mother, you knew about it and you lied to help him cover up his crime. Because of you, he's escaped justice all these years."

Betsy's cheeks reddened. "Now, listen here..."

"Come on, Mum. Let's go and see if there's still some of that delicious leg ham left. We can make a sandwich and I'll get you a ginger beer. You'll feel better in no time."

With one last flash of defiance in her eyes, Ruby took Penny's hand and hobbled with her towards the food tables, with Henry following behind them. Penny felt strangely calm. She'd feared a conflict would happen, but now that it had, found it wasn't so bad. They'd all survived and there was a certain amount of satisfaction in her mother taking the opportunity to speak her mind, something she'd probably never done before.

Penny found a plate and began piling it with food for her mother. Ruby caught her gaze and Penny began to giggle. She knew it was wrong, but she couldn't help it. The sight of her petite, elderly mother, calling June Clements a hussy was too much to bear.

"You really let them have it, Mum."

Ruby laughed, her cheeks red. "Well, everything I said was true."

"You should've seen the look on June's face. She was fuming."

They both laughed heartily then, until neither one of them had any laughter left inside.

"I've been wanting to say those things for so long. It feels good to get it out of my system." Ruby raised a hand to her chest. "I'm lighter somehow."

"That's great, Mum." Penny wound an arm around her mother's slight shoulders. "But please, no mud wrestling today. That's where I draw the line."

* * *

The rest of the party flew by, and Penny managed to keep her family on their best behaviour. Her parents avoided June and Betsy. Her brother, Rob, made amends with their mother. Rowan manned the barbecue and kept all the guests well stocked with rissoles and sausages to eat. The sun continued to shine, even as clouds gathered and darkened on the horizon. The water sparkled blue and clear. The yacht was constantly crowded with swimmers and sunbathers. Penny made small talk, ensured everyone felt welcome, handed out drinks, topped up cups, and ferried plates of food to fill all those bellies.

Finally, after her family and Rowan's left, she collapsed in a chair with a sigh. The adrenaline quickly faded from her system, and she was exhausted. Rowan sat beside her, his chef's hat crooked and his apron smeared with grease.

"That was intense," he said.

She laughed tiredly. "It went well though, apart from that one fight. Don't you think?"

"It was great." He leaned over to kiss her cheek. "You did a fantastic job, honey. Everyone had a lovely time."

"Thanks for all the cooking you did."

"My pleasure." He grinned. "It gave me something to do."

She yawned. "I could sleep right here in this spot."

"I'll start packing up the chairs."

"Be right with you," Penny said without moving an inch.

He laughed and wandered off to join Rob and Aidan, who were already stacking chairs into the back of Aidan's ute.

Taya covered the remnants of the coleslaw with a lid. "The potato salad is completely gone. I think someone might've even licked the bowl. And we didn't even have to resort to using it as a weapon."

Penny giggled. "Thanks for bringing it. Your salads are always a hit."

"You're very welcome. I'm glad I could contribute in some way." She sat beside them, leaving the salads on the table. "I can't believe you're finally getting married."

"I know—it's surreal. All these years, I honestly thought I'd missed the boat, that it was never going to happen. And I was okay with that. I'd come to terms with it a long time ago. I didn't expect to find love now, and certainly not with Rowan Clements." She chuckled. "Isn't it funny, the twists and turns life can take?"

"I know what you mean," Taya replied. "I couldn't have imagined selling the inn."

"How do you feel about it now that the dust has settled?"

"Like a weight has been lifted from my shoulders and the entire world is open to me. I could do anything, live anywhere, change careers... I'm overwhelmed by possibility." She shrugged. "I've applied for a new job within the company."

"Doing what?"

"I'd be travelling around to resort locations, helping new resorts get established, ensuring older resorts are well maintained and fit our brand image. I'd also be mentoring local women into management positions."

"Wow. That sounds perfect for you." Penny straightened. "Will you get it? I'm sure you will. It's your father's company."

"I don't know. I suppose if he doesn't think I'm ready for the job, he might give it to someone else. But I'm hopeful."

"Sounds like we'll be seeing even less of you, though."

Taya smiled. "That's true, but we'll still be able to have our girls' lunches."

"We can fit them around your schedule."

"That would be lovely." Taya sighed. "I've got the interview in a few days' time. I'm actually pretty nervous. I haven't done many interviews, and I'm sure there'll be some really impressive people applying."

"You'll kill it," Penny reassured her.

"Then there's Andrew."

"What about him?"

"We've only recently begun seeing each other, and it's going well. He's fantastic. But if I take this job, I'll be travelling all the time, and we won't see as much of each other. I could end up torpedoing the relationship before it's had a chance to develop." She ran fingers over her elegant bob, smoothing flyaway strands into place.

Penny cocked her head to one side. "Well, that might be true. But if Andrew is the right man for you, he'll understand what you're doing and why, and he'll support you."

"You're right, of course. I don't know why I'm so worried about it. He's not the kind of man to become insecure about us because I'm not here every day."

"No, it doesn't seem as though he is, although I've only met him once. I think it's important that you do what you want to do with your life. You've spent the past twenty years raising a child on your own, running a very demanding inn. It's your time now." Penny reached out to pat her arm. "Don't worry about what everyone else needs. Think about what you'd like to do. Life doesn't last forever. What's important to you?"

"I really want to do this. I think it'll help me better understand the business. And if I take over, like Dad wants me to, I need to be in touch with all of the resorts. I should also be networking with managers and listening to their needs. This would be a great way to do that."

"I agree," Penny said. "It's the right time and the right job."

"So, I shouldn't overthink it."

"No, you shouldn't." Penny would miss spending so much time with Taya, but her lifelong friend was transforming into the strong, confident woman Penny had always known she had the potential to become. "You should go for it."

After everything had been packed into vehicles, the beach-front was as pristine as if they'd never been there. Penny and Rowan climbed into her car and drove back to the beach house together. Rob was already at home, watching a football game on the television in the living room, so she and Rowan sat out on the porch with a cold drink to watch the colours from the setting sun dancing across the ocean's darkening surface.

"You still want to marry me? Even if family gatherings end up looking like a boxing match?" Rowan asked, his eyes twinkling.

She leaned over to press her lips to his, then collapsed back into her chair. "More than ever."

"Glad to hear it."

"Every single muscle in my body aches. Remind me never to run a party like that on my own again. If we throw another one that size, we're hiring someone to cater it."

He laughed. "Good idea. If only someone had suggested that…"

"I know you said we should get it catered, but I thought the personal touch would make all the difference."

"And you were right," he admitted. "It was a lot of work, but the atmosphere was very warm, loving and fun. We'll remember it for the rest of our lives."

"I'm going to head to bed," she said, standing to her feet.

"It's only seven," Rowan objected. "Don't you want to stay out here a little longer? Maybe get some dinner?"

"I can't keep my eyes open."

"You've been tired a lot lately. Are you sure you're okay? There's nothing going on with your health, is there?"

She rubbed her eyes with her fingertips. "No, I'm fine. I've been staying up late at night doing paperwork, that's all. There's so much to do and not enough hours in the day to get it done."

She'd always struggled with the administrative side of running the refuge. But lately things had gotten even worse — her part-time administrative assistant resigned a couple of months earlier. On top of that, since she'd received the government grant, their workload had only increased.

Rowan reached out for her hand. He pulled her to the railing and leaned against it, then wrapped her in his arms. "I've been meaning to talk to you about something. Don't feel pressured at all to do it, but it's a suggestion."

She tipped her head back to look into his eyes. "What is it?"

"You're so busy, and I'm looking for a way to stay on the island and give up my job. Maybe we could work together."

Her heart skipped a beat. Could they work together? What if it destroyed their connection? She could be difficult, emotional—even demanding at times. He might not like that about her. And then where would they stand?

"Together?"

"I could help do the administrative tasks for the refuge and take that off your hands. You could focus on managing the place and caring for the animals. It's only an idea, so don't feel as though you have to make a decision right now. I won't be offended if you'd rather not. But I thought this might be a way for me to be home more while helping you at the same time."

"It would help me..."

He caressed her back, his hands moving in circles. "We could spend so much more time together. What do you think?"

She looped her arms around his neck and pushed up onto her tiptoes to kiss him. His lips were warm and soft on hers. She was so excited that she would get to spend the rest of her life with this man.

"I think it's a fantastic idea, but I also think you're making so many big changes in your life already. I worry this might be one too many for you. It won't be much of a challenge compared with what you're used to spending your days doing..."

"I thought I'd probably keep up with some freelance work for the local papers on the mainland. But I'm ready to slow things down and settle in one place for a while."

"But what if you grow to resent me? Or get sick of me?"

"I'll let you know immediately and send you packing," he said with a grin.

She pouted. "I'm serious."

"So am I," he replied, kissing the end of her nose. "We'll talk. All the time. If things change, if I find I'm getting restless, I promise to tell you. Does that make you feel better?"

"Yes," she admitted. "I like the sound of that."

"So, will you hire me?"

"As long as you're not inappropriate with the boss."

He laughed. "You're foiling my plan."

Five

⮜⮝

LIVING in the small apartment above the florist shop was everything Charmaine had hoped for. It was quaint, cosy and best of all, free. Betsy had given her an old rusty bike to help her get around the island as soon as she realised Charmaine was traveling on foot. She'd told her the island was too big to manage without wheels and that she didn't ride anymore, so she had no need of the contraption.

A couple of new tyres and a pump had been all it took to get the bike into riding shape. The care and concern Charmaine had already encountered in the short time she'd lived on Coral Island had surprised her in the best possible way. She felt as though she'd stepped onto a Hallmark movie set.

There was only one problem. She was completely alone. She loved that she'd met so many friendly acquaintances since she arrived, but she didn't have family or close friends to share her life with. Or to tell her secrets, to complain about her hard day, to commiserate over an aching back from lifting so many boxes or stooping over vases of flowers at the market.

No one to laugh with over bad dates—not that she'd had any kind of date in years. Or to set her up with a cute coworker who'd turn out to be a bore intent on lecturing her over cock-tails on the benefits of crypto currencies, as her last blind date back in Newcastle had done. She had to break it to him that she didn't really possess any kind of currency, let alone crypto, nor did she understand what it was, even after he patiently and then impatiently explained it to her. To this day, she still couldn't understand why anyone would use real money to buy pretend money. But when she'd calmly relayed that opinion to him, he'd retreated into a huff, implied that she was simple minded, and the rest of the date had been a disaster.

Loneliness wasn't anything new for Charmaine. She'd been alone for three years, ever since her mother died. She assumed her brother lived somewhere in Melbourne or Adelaide. She wasn't exactly sure, since he'd left after their mother died and hadn't stayed in touch. Even before her death, he'd been absent more than he'd been present. He'd visited them every now and then, mostly at the holidays. But he wasn't good at keeping contact, and for much of that time she was a teenager, too caught up in her own life to notice.

He'd returned to Newcastle to live with her in their family home when their mother got sick. She'd been grateful for that. It was hard on her — studying, taking Mum to her appoint-ments, paying the bills. Especially when Mum got so bad that she couldn't manage her job. That was when things got really tough and Sean had stepped up, helping her pay the mortgage and buying groceries when they needed them. It'd surprised her how much concern he'd shown, since they'd barely heard from him in over a year and even then he'd forgotten to bring a gift to their Christmas celebration.

But he became a doting son and brother at the last moment, and Charmaine had learned to rely on him in a way she hadn't relied on anyone other than her mother for her entire life. One of the mantras Mum had taught her early in life was *We've only got each other and we don't need anyone else.*

It'd been the two of them against the world for so many years that Charmaine wasn't entirely sure how to make room for Sean at first. But then she didn't have much of a choice and she quickly grew accustomed to his being there.

In the end, it was a series of strokes that took her from them, and the doctors still couldn't give them a definitive reason why. It hardly mattered after the fact. Charmaine had been so mired in grief and pain, she'd become quite numb. She'd dropped out of university weeks earlier, when it all became too much. Instead of returning to her studies, as soon as her mother's funeral was over and her affairs in order, Charmaine left Newcastle behind and didn't look back once.

What broke her heart all over again was the fact that Sean disappeared within days of her mother's death. Right when she needed his help to pull together a service to celebrate her life. Right when she was finding it difficult to put one foot in front of the other. Right when she was fielding calls from creditors and solicitors about bills owed and estates to manage, he was gone. She called his phone for days, but finally it responded with the out-of-service tone and she knew—he wasn't coming back.

When Sean didn't show up for their mother's funeral, she'd been devastated all over again. But several basic internet searches didn't give her any clue about his location. He was a programmer and paranoid about his digital footprint, so had never opened any social media accounts.

None of his childhood friends seemed to know where he was. But that was hardly surprising, since he'd fallen out of contact with most of them years earlier. From what Charmaine could tell, he hadn't made any new friends while staying in Newcastle. There were people he spent time with, but she didn't know them by name and couldn't find any contact details.

They had no other family worth mentioning, so there was

no one to call and no one for him to bunk with even if he'd been so inclined. Given her own state of mind, she didn't search for him long. She had enough to deal with without worrying herself over a brother who clearly didn't care enough about her to be there for her when she needed him most.

She was all alone in the world, apart from a few scattered distant relatives. And certainly all alone on Coral Island. She lay on the daybed against the window that looked out onto the road. A mound of pillows behind her head meant she was propped up enough to watch the comings and goings of the locals on Kellyville's Main Street. It was the only way she had, on her day off, to connect with someone other than the characters in the book that was spread open in her lap.

She stared at the book cover, sighed, picked it up and continued reading. The mood she was in wasn't conducive to falling deep into a story, but she wasn't sure what else to do with her time off. She wasn't much into using her computer or her phone since she hadn't no one to contact and would likely end up doomscrolling through worthless content that would make her feel worse about her own life.

There was a scratching noise at the other end of the apartment. An external door led to a set of steps that ran down the outside of the building. She rarely used those steps. She mostly entered her unit via the florist shop. It made her feel more secure, since the steps were internal and less exposed.

The scratching happened again. It sent a shiver up her spine. There were no trees on that side of the flat, so the noise couldn't have come from a tree branch against the siding.

The sound happened again. She swung her legs over the side of the bed with a frown. What was that? Had it come from someone's fingernails? What if there was an axe murderer waiting outside her door, hoping she'd open it? He could push by her into the flat and kill her. Would anyone know? If she screamed, who would hear her? There were shops on either side of her building, and as far as she knew, there weren't any other flats nearby. And given the time of day, most of the shops were likely to be shut. Her scalp tingled, and goose bumps broke out along her arms. Surely no one would run their fingernails over a stranger's door. That would be utterly creepy.

Another scratch.

She tiptoed across the flat, adrenaline spiking and eyes wide. When she reached the back door, she tugged aside the thin curtains that hung across a large window in the top of the door and peered out. There was no one there.

She sighed with relief. Perhaps she'd imagined the sound. Or maybe it was coming from somewhere else. Then it happened again, right under her nose. She pushed her face to the window and looked down. A grey cat with its tail held high turned a circle on the landing, then stared up at her. She smiled, her heart rate slowing back to a normal pace.

"Kitty! You scared the life out of me."

She was about to return to her book when the scratch came again. She glanced down and noticed there was a cat door set into the larger door. It was locked and painted the same colour as the rest of the door.

She squatted before it and tugged at the peg that locked it shut. With a bit of effort, the peg shifted, and the door swung slightly back and forth in place. When she took a step back, the grey cat pushed through and rubbed itself around her legs in a figure of eight, purring.

She gaped. "Oh, hi. Uh... How did you know about that door? And where did you come from?"

The cat looked up at her, then continued rubbing against her legs, purring.

"Why am I asking you questions, waiting you to come up with some kind of answer?" She shook her head. "Maybe I'm losing my mind. I've been alone for so long that now I'm talking to animals and expecting to have a conversation."

She bent down to stroke the cat along its back, and it rose to meet her hand in a snake-like movement. Its fur was soft to the touch, and she noticed it wore a collar with a small bell attached, along with a tag. She read the tag.

"Watson. That's a pretty great name."

The cat wandered off into the unit, then bounded up onto her armchair and curled into the seat, tail wrapped around his lithe frame.

"Make yourself at home," Charmaine said, one eyebrow arched. She'd never owned an animal, and she wasn't sure if this was normal cat behaviour. But he certainly seemed to have been there before—he acted as though the unit was very familiar and he was as comfortable there as anywhere.

"Are you hungry? I'm sure you'd eat if I had food to give you. Now, what would a cat enjoy?" She rummaged around in the small cabinet that served as her pantry, looking for something the creature might eat. She found a can of tuna and flicked the lid open, then spooned the contents into a bowl. "Here you go. I'll bet you like fish, huh? Come and have some tuna, Watson."

The cat leapt down from the armchair and ran to the bowl, then bowed his head to eat. He didn't hesitate and immediately began licking up pieces of tuna, grasping at the fish with his teeth. He soon settled down in front of the bowl, eating and then occasionally glancing up at her with curiosity in his green eyes.

"Where did you come from?" Charmaine mused. She sat on the floor beside the cat while it ate and reached gently for his collar again. Turning the name tag over, she discovered a phone number. Should she call the owner to let them know she had their cat? She wasn't sure about the etiquette for cat owners, but presumed the animal would find his way home on his own once it was finished with the tuna.

In the end, she relented and sent the number a text message to let them know Watson was with her and she'd fed him tuna. She ended the message with *your neighbour, Chaz*. She received a message almost immediately telling her that it was fine, Watson was a wanderer and would come home when he was ready, but to kick him out if he became a pain. The person signed off with *official cat owner, Finn*.

Finn — could be a male or female name. She'd had a female friend in high school who was a Finn—they'd played on the netball team together. Well, whoever Finn was, wherever he lived, he'd named his cat Watson, so he must be a Sherlock Holmes fan and that was good enough for Charmaine. She hoped it was the books that Finn enjoyed, which were far superior in every way to the movies and TV show, although she'd enjoyed them as well.

She stroked the cat's head, and he purred, licking his chops. "You couldn't ever be a pain. Could you, Watson?" she whispered.

A few minutes later, Charmaine decided to take a walk. The sun would be setting soon, and she needed to get out of the tiny flat and stretch her legs. She'd taken a swim that morning but had spent the rest of the day lounging about the room, reading books and eating. It was time to breathe some fresh air.

She waved goodbye to Watson, reminded him of the swinging cat door should he wish to leave, then headed out through the internal staircase and the empty, darkened florist shop. A sound at the back of the shop, in the storage room or kitchen, caught her attention.

She hesitated halfway across the floor, then turned and tiptoed back. She should leave it alone and go upstairs to look at the security footage. Betsy had installed cameras well before

Charmaine arrived on the island and had given her access to view the footage on her phone. But she'd left her phone on her bed.

With a shake of her head and heart pounding, she crept forwards. Perhaps it was a giant rat. She didn't have any desire to confront a rodent. Although she did have a cat upstairs that might do the job. Maybe Watson would come in handy as a rat catcher.

Charmaine peered around the edge of the doorframe. Her gaze took in the opening to the kitchen—she couldn't see all the way in—then down the hallway. She tiptoed forwards, careful not to make a sound, her breath caught in her throat. Finally, she scanned the storage room at the end of the hall. A piece of paper fluttered to the floor. Then a pile of folders crashed onto the ground. Her eyes widened. What on earth was going on?

Perhaps she should call Betsy, although she should get a little closer look if she was going to relay to her boss what was happening. As far as she knew, no one but she or Betsy had a key or the security code to get into the building. But she hadn't been there long enough to know for certain. Maybe someone else was allowed in and had the kind of filing system that involved hurling folders through the air before organising them.

As she slunk along the corridor, a photograph wafted down through the air and drifted into the storage room doorway. A photograph of a dancer in black and white. The photo was marked and scuffed, and torn at one corner. It looked much like the photos Betsy had hung around the cash register at the back of the shop.

Charmaine's throat was dry. She couldn't hear much other than the pounding of her own heart. She pressed up to the side of the doorframe and peeked around for a brief moment, then withdrew again. Her eyes narrowed. It was Betsy — she stood in the centre of the storage room where a table was strewn with files, paper, photographs and folders. Her back was to Charmaine, and she was riffling through the paperwork, tossing things left and right over her shoulders.

It didn't make sense. Why would Betsy come in on a Sunday in order to make a mess of her own files? Charmaine crept back down the corridor and out through the florist shop to the street beyond. Long shadows cooled the street. Shoppers wandered up and down its length. The sun had drifted behind the buildings, throwing the island into a growing twilight. She released the breath she'd been holding in her chest, then broke into a jog.

When she'd first met Betsy, she'd liked her immediately. She was elderly but vital. Her eyes sparked with life and humour. She'd built a beautiful shop and was willing not only to give Charmaine flexible working hours, but also provide a place to live. But over the past few weeks, since she'd been on the island, she'd noticed a few strange things about Betsy. Her relationship with her son, for one. And sometimes she seemed so distracted. She'd hidden something beneath her desk a couple of times when Charmaine came into the room. And now this. Something was going on with her boss.

She ran for as long as the light held out along the shoreline. It was already dark when she made her way back up the stairs to her silent unit. Watson was gone, so she locked the cat door and flicked on a light switch. The apartment seemed lonely without the cat stretched out on her armchair. With a sigh, she opened the refrigerator to scan its shelves for something to eat. Finding nothing interesting, she threw herself into the chair with a grunt. She needed to go shopping, but it was hard to be motivated when she had only herself to feed. Perhaps she should buy some cat food.

Six

THE NIGHT AIR was cool on Bea's skin as she gently steered the boat through the bay. They'd slowed their pace as they neared the foreshore at Airlie Beach, and the scarf around her hair had stopped flapping as the wind abated. The sky was dark, just. The last remnants of sunlight glinted on the horizon beyond the town. Streetlights and sparkling windows dotted the hillsides like stars in an inky night.

Airlie Beach was a beautiful little hamlet, sitting cosy along the shoreline. It swelled in size during tourist season, but the rest of the year was sleepy and quiet. The shore had been turned into a tropical paradise, with a quaint sandy beach, palm trees winding along a wide footpath and sculptures here and there.

Beyond the foreshore, a sweet little central street housed touristy shops, fashion boutiques and restaurants and clubs, as well as an array of palm trees, shrubs and garden beds, all meticulously maintained. On the other side of the headland was the marina, large and spacious, with yachts and boats of varying sizes moored throughout. That was where Bea was headed as she turned the rudder to steer her small boat around the point and into the marina to dock. Her brother leased several spaces along one dock and had offered to let her use it whenever she wished.

In the boat, Penny, Taya and Eveleigh all sat along the bench seats on either side of the rear, behind where Bea stood. They'd given up on conversation as soon as they'd left the island — the noise of the engine, the wind, the slapping of small waves against the hull were too much for them to hear each other's voices. But as she pulled into the dock, they started chatting again.

They were all excited about an evening out on the town. Now that Bea lived on the island, she understood the need to visit a larger town or city every now and then. Coral Island was the perfect getaway from the noise and bustle of the mainland life, but sometimes it was good to immerse herself in the buzz of it all. She missed the energy of life in the city on occasion, but Airlie Beach was nothing like a city. For tonight, it would have to do.

"Ready for your hen's night?" she asked as she switched off the boat engine.

Taya tied the boat to the dock. Eveleigh and Penny climbed out of the boat hand in hand.

Penny straightened the glowing headband that flashed the word *bride* atop her head with a grin. "I'm ready to party!"

Bea's smile faded. "I'm not sure if we're going to do a lot of partying..."

Penny laughed. "What I mean is, I'm ready to eat rich Mexican food, take an antacid and go to bed early. Better?"

Taya rolled her eyes. "You guys. Come on—how often does one of us get married?"

"For me?" Penny shrugged. "Never before."

"Right, so let's do this — it's celebration time."

"The middle-aged way..." Eveleigh added, raising both hands in the air. "With orthotics and regular hydration."

Bea laughed. "Come on, ladies. We can be young again for one night. It's all for a good cause. Besides, it's been so long since I went out after dark, I feel like I'm becoming a recluse."

"Reclusive with Aidan Whitlock," Taya murmured with a wink. "You poor thing."

They all laughed then.

Bea had been looking forward to the evening all week long, but she'd woken up with sciatic pain in her lower back and right hip, and she hadn't slept well because of it. So she was exhausted and a little on edge, but spending time with her friends was just the thing she needed to get her laughing and to help her forget about the twinge in her hip. Besides, it was Penny's big night. Time to push aside her own feelings and have a wonderful time for her friend's sake if for no other reason.

She hobbled along the dock after them, wishing she'd worn pants instead of a flimsy dress. It'd been almost impossible to hold down while driving the boat, and now that she was on the shore, the wind came in gusts, lifting the fabric into the air around her every few seconds.

"Ugh, this is ridiculous." She pushed one hand down on the dress, the other clutching her small purse.

"We can stop along the way to the restaurant and buy you some leggings if you like," Eveleigh suggested.

Bea frowned. "Really? I don't want to be a buzzkill, but that would help a lot. I'd love not to flash my undies at the entire town."

"It's no problem at all. We're early for our reservation anyway." Taya looped her arm through Penny's. "Mexican food, followed by dancing. Does that sound okay?"

"It's perfect," Penny replied. "Mexican is my favourite."

"I know," Taya said with a laugh. "But really, who doesn't like Mexican food? And this little place on the foreshore is amazing. You're going to love it. They do a taco salad that's to die for."

"Salad? Really?" Penny asked. "It's not a salad kind of night."

"I forgot," Taya said, patting Penny's arm. "You're a melted cheese and chips kind of gal."

"All day long — I know it's not healthy, but sometimes you've got to enjoy life. In fact, I insist we all get dessert as well. No diets tonight!"

"After a couple of cocktails, I'll be downing gelato like I'm in Rome," Bea replied with a chuckle, doing her best not to grimace from the tweaking pain in her hip with every step she took. "Although since I'm the designated driver, I suppose they'll be virgin cocktails anyway. So never mind."

"Are you okay?" Eveleigh asked, concern etched on her face.

"Yep, fine," Bea replied in a tight voice.

They stopped at several small boutiques along the esplanade on their way to the restaurant and browsed through silk kaftans, skimpy bikinis, sarongs and the shortest shorts Bea had ever seen. Finally, she found a pair of black leggings in a small bin in the back of one boutique, purchased a pair and pulled them on in the change room beneath her dress. She joined the others, who'd all made purchases as well, and they linked arms to walk down the street together.

"It's so good to get away from everything," Penny said. "Did I tell you that Rowan wants to work at the refuge with me?"

"Wow. Really?" Taya asked.

"That's a great idea," Bea said.

"What do you think about it?" Eveleigh asked.

Penny sighed. "It's amazing, and he's wonderful for suggesting it. But what if it ruins our relationship? I don't know if we'd be able to work together. I can be a bit irritating at times. I'm sure my staff would say that's an understatement. But they have to put up with me because I'm their boss."

"You're not *completely* irritating," Taya replied. "Not all the time, anyway."

"Gee, thanks for the ringing endorsement," Penny sassed.

"The sarcasm *is* irritating, though," Taya said with a shake of her head and a sparkle in her eye.

"You're hilarious. I'm being serious — I want to work with him. I need the help since I have far more work than I can manage, but I don't want to cause tension between us."

"It might cause tension at some point," Bea said. "But once you're married, that's going to happen eventually anyway. You'll have to learn to navigate living together and dealing with conflict in your relationship as a couple whether you work together or not."

"That's true," Penny admitted. "If we can't manage this, we won't be able to manage living in the same house."

"I say give it a go. If it doesn't work, you can always make a change," Eveleigh suggested.

They arrived at the Mexican restaurant. Night had fallen, and there were people everywhere. Restaurants were packed with patrons. Nightclubs and bars had revellers spilling out of doorways. Music blared, and the rhythmic beat of drums escaped to echo along the footpath. The heady scent of a multitude of different types of foods, along with vape smoke and alcohol, filled the air.

"Here we are," Taya said, leading the way inside.

The restaurant was decorated with Mexican artwork, pictures of colourful cottages with statues of beautiful women and clay pots. There were twinkle lights hanging from rafters overhead, and soft mariachi music played through speakers around the room.

They sat at a small table in the back of the restaurant and reminisced over their teen years together. Taya gave a small speech about Penny and Rowan, and they all said cheers and clinked glasses then drank. Bea ate the taco salad and Taya was right, it was delicious. She poured herself a glass of red wine to go with it, since it paired perfectly and brought out the flavours in a new way.

Taya ordered the chicken enchiladas, Eveleigh had a burrito, and Penny of course had an enormous beef nachos. They enjoyed chips with salsa throughout the evening and finished with churros and caramel dipping sauce for dessert. By the time they were done, Bea was completely stuffed full and glad to be able to get to her feet and limp from the restaurant out into the cool night air.

"Are you hurt?" Taya asked, slipping her arm through Bea's.

"Sciatic pain. It's no big deal."

"Do you think you can still go dancing?"

She forced a smile onto her face. "Of course. I'm looking forward to it."

"I don't think anyone would mind if you wanted to call it a night. I'm already tired. I don't know how we used to stay out at the clubs until dawn." Taya yawned. "All that food in my stomach... I could curl up on the couch and go to sleep."

"You two aren't being spoilsports, are you?" Eveleigh shouted back at them over her shoulder.

"No, we're ready to dance the night away." Taya winked at Beatrice.

They found a small club up a winding staircase on the second level above a tapas restaurant. Trance-style dance music slammed through the door when Bea opened it. They stayed close as they made their way across the club. It was packed with people, and several times, Bea thought she might lose her group as dancers pushed up against her, blocking her path. The music was so loud, she couldn't hear her own thoughts.

They danced for several hours, and despite her pain, Bea

had a good time. She'd forgotten what it felt like to abandon herself to the music, to forget about her responsibilities and let herself get caught up in the moment. When Penny finally said that she'd had enough, they all grabbed a drink of water from the bar and headed back to the boat. Along the way, Penny got her heel caught in between two planks on the boardwalk. It tore off, and she had to remove her shoes so she didn't have to hobble all the way through the marina.

Bea walked beside her, the cool night air bringing her back to reality and reminding her of all the problems waiting for her at home — the café, Dani's new boyfriend, Buck's impending murder trial. There were so many things on her mind, sometimes it was difficult to switch off and simply enjoy the here and now.

"Have you heard anything else about Buck's trial?"

Penny nodded. "No good news though, I'm afraid."

"What's going on?" Taya asked.

"The bail hearing is coming up, and the police think the magistrate will let him out since he has ties to the community."

"That's not good," Eveleigh said. "What if he kills someone else?"

"Like the person who found evidence against him?" Bea added with wide eyes.

Penny patted her arm. "Apparently they weren't able to break his alibi. Betsy's sticking to it, even though she all but admitted she lied to you. They say she's not backing down."

"That's so frustrating," Bea said.

"It seems their case isn't as rock solid as we'd thought," Penny added with a shrug. "But all we can do is trust in the system to work the way it's supposed to."

"I'm sure this is hard for you," Eveleigh said sympathetically. "He is your father, after all."

"Very true," Penny said. "I'd love nothing more than to be

completely and utterly mistaken about him. He seemed so lovely when we met. And now, to think he was the one who killed my grandmother — I hope we're all wrong."

"But it doesn't seem likely, does it?" Taya asked.

"No, it doesn't."

As they climbed into the boat to return home, Bea's mind was troubled. Very soon there might well be a murderer loose on Coral Island. One who most likely knew she'd turned him in and found evidence against him. What would that mean? Was her life in danger?

Seven

TULLE, lace and gold ribbons lay in clumps around the floor of Charmaine's tiny unit. She tidied a stack of invitations and leaned against the chair behind her with a sigh. Her back was killing her. She pressed both hands to it, leaned one way then the other, doing her best to work out the knots.

She rubbed her eyes with her fingertips. Penny's wedding was coming together well so far. She hadn't realised just how much work would be involved when she signed up to plan it, but even with the amount of stress it'd brought into her life, she was still glad she'd taken the chance.

The flower shop had been busier than usual lately. There were weddings on the island every weekend. Charmaine's schedule was packed with appointments, trips to the markets with Betsy to look at flowers, processing purchase orders, and deliveries. The emotion of wedding preparations always made everything more stressful and heated. It was inevitable that something would go wrong, or a bride would be unhappy over an arrangement, or a particular flower would be unobtainable.

Whenever things went south, it was always Betsy's job to step in and smooth things over with the client. Charmaine didn't know how she managed to stay so composed through it all, but she'd already learned a lot about dealing with difficult personalities and crises from her boss.

She'd enjoyed planning Penny's wedding on top of all her other responsibilities, but it meant that she'd barely stopped in recent days. She needed a break. To get outside and see the sunshine. She wasn't the type who liked to stay cooped up indoors for too long. Her favourite part of each day was when she left the confines of the flat and headed out for a walk, a ride or a swim.

She loved that she could ride her bike ten minutes to reach an amazing snorkelling location with a brilliantly coloured small coral reef and tropical fish. With golden sands, ever present sunshine—apart from the occasional tropical storm or downpour—and a small-town feel that gave her a sense of satisfaction and belonging she'd never had before, Coral Island was fast becoming her home. Already she was beginning to feel better about her life and the prospects the future held.

When she'd fled Newcastle after her mother's death, a sense of foreboding had crept into her heart — the prospect of a future alone and eking out a living doing minimum-wage work was all she had to look forward to. She'd wondered many times how she would make it. The years stretched ahead of her, empty and bleak. But now, even though she was still alone, she didn't feel quite so lonely. When she'd walked down Main Street the day before, she'd had five different people greet her. It warmed her heart to think about it even now. They'd accepted her as one of them.

She dressed in her swimsuit, slipped her helmet onto her head and wheeled the bike down the back staircase. The tyres bumped on each step. Then she climbed aboard, her small bag of snorkelling gear on her back, and pedalled away.

It didn't take long to leave the town behind. Her hair blew back over her shoulders in the wind. There wasn't a single car on the road. Her nostrils filled with the scent of salt and sunshine. She grinned as she crested a hill, then raised her feet high as the bike picked up speed down the other side.

Betsy had given her the afternoon off, since they didn't have much going on. She'd done all the prep work for the upcoming week, and Betsy had declared she didn't know how she'd managed before Charmaine came along. Charmaine had fought back the tears at her words. Encouragement over a job well done, appreciation for her hard work—these were things she wasn't accustomed to receiving. Betsy was an encourager. Even when Charmaine made mistakes, Betsy rarely admonished her, instead taking the opportunity to point out something good she'd done instead.

That afternoon, Betsy and Sam were both camped out in the shop, doing homework and baking brownies in the small kitchen. Betsy said they didn't need Charmaine and since she'd put in so many extra hours lately, she should go out and enjoy herself.

"You're only young once, honey," she'd stated with a wink.

Charmaine sometimes felt as though she'd never really been young. She was an old soul living in a young body, or something like that. At least, that's what Mum used to say when the two of them would sit and play a game of chess on a Sunday afternoon, or would read, side by side, in their swinging hammocks late into the evening.

"Why don't you go out with some friends your own age?" Mum had asked on more than one occasion.

But Charmaine had simply shrugged and turned the page of her book. "I do sometimes, but I like being here with you. It's my favourite thing to do."

Mum would laugh at that. "But we're not really doing anything."

"Exactly," Charmaine would reply.

Then the two of them would chuckle together before

falling back into quiet reading in their garden, bees humming around them, birds twittering, and mosquitos readying themselves in the hedgerows for the moment the sun dipped beyond the horizon.

Afternoon and early evening were Charmaine's favourite times of the day. She usually finished work by five, and with the autumn days still long, she could often stay out swimming until sundown and riding until well after seven. The heat of the day was no longer oppressive by afternoon, and she enjoyed the cool breeze that picked up over the ocean and gently buffeted the island each day.

The cove where she snorkelled came into view quickly, and she aimed the bike to the left to follow the potholed track that veered away from the road between two tall gum trees, their smoky green leaves shushing in the wind as the tallest branches swayed to a steady rhythm.

A tiny brown dog rushed at Charmaine's bike, barking furiously. She swerved to miss it, and her bike struck a tree root. Then the front tyre landed in a soft patch of sand, dug in, and she went hurtling over the handlebars. She landed on her back in the sand with a thud. The wind was knocked from her lungs, and she lay still a moment, staring up at the sky, her mouth opening and closing like a goldfish. Suddenly all the world rushed in at her, banishing her sense of goodwill. There was no pain, and no air. Then the feeling passed, and she heaved in a big breath.

"Oh, my goodness. Are you okay? Fudge, that was very naughty. Look what you did." Beatrice Rushton hurried over to Charmaine and helped her sit. Then, she stared at her worriedly until Charmaine was able to stand to her feet with a wobbly smile.

"I'm okay. Nothing broken. At least, it doesn't seem so. Maybe I'm still in shock, though."

It was meant as a joke, but Bea's frown only deepened and

she wrung her hands together. "I told you not to run off like that," she scolded the dog. She was puffing lightly, and a pair of sunglasses sat on top of her head as though she'd pushed them there in a hurry. Her hair was askew and spiked above the glasses in all directions. "I'm sorry, Chaz, but Fudge can be very wilful, and he decided to chase a bird. Then you came along on your bike, and I'm afraid he thought it was all a big game."

"It's fine." Charmaine bent to pat the dog's head. The animal immediately resorted to licking her hand all over. A leash was attached to a red collar and lay coiled in the sand beside the dog.

Bea picked up the leash and looped it around her hand. "Now you can't get away from me."

"What are you doing here?" Charmaine asked, raising a hand to shield her eyes from the sun as she regarded the cove, the sparkling water and the clear blue sky overhead. It was a perfect day for snorkelling, and she was more than ready to get started. Her entire body was covered in a film of sweat and now a layer of sand and grit after her tumble.

"Aiden and I came down for a quick swim after work. Are you swimming?"

"I'm going to snorkel."

"Oh, perfect. It's lovely here. And I promise to keep Fudge well away."

"I don't mind," Charmaine replied, tickling Fudge under the chin. "I love animals. I only swerved because I didn't want to run over him. I'm still not great on the bike yet. It's been a long time since I owned one."

"Do you have any pets?"

She considered the empty unit above the floral shop, her heart constricting. "No."

"Maybe you should get one. They're great company." Bea's voice was compassionate.

"There is a cat." She pressed a half smile to her face. "He came in through my pet door. He's not mine, but seems to think he owns the place. He visited me a few days ago, and now he keeps coming back at the same time every afternoon. I've been feeding him — so that's probably why."

"What's he look like?" Bea asked.

"Grey with green eyes."

"Oh, that's Watson."

"How did you know?" Charmaine asked.

Bea laughed. "He used to visit the previous resident, a woman who worked for Betsy years ago. Watson's family got a dog recently. The kids are loving it, but he's not very happy about the new arrangement. He's been doing the rounds—he even comes by the café and makes himself at home sometimes. I have a little bowl I put milk into when he looks hungry. He's not feeling the love at home anymore and has taken to searching elsewhere for it."

Charmaine smiled, but inside she identified with the cat even more. She'd never felt so feline in her life. Watson was lonely and rejected, and so was she. Perhaps Watson was grieving too — the loss of his status as king of the castle, the peace and tranquility of a dog-free home.

Whatever it was that'd pushed him to explore other options, she understood the need to find a place of his own. Somewhere he could relax and be at peace, without worrying about the past, or what others might think. They were alike, the two of them—perhaps that's why he'd settled into her flat so easily. She'd decided after his first visit to leave the cat door unlocked so he could come and go as he pleased, and he'd been to visit her almost every day since.

Charmaine rested her bike against a tree, grateful to see there was no damage done by her fall. Then she followed Bea and Fudge down the winding, sandy path to the small beach in the cove. The cove itself was hidden by a thicket of bushes and trees — gums and she-oaks, seagrass and wildflowers. Rainbow lorikeets and rosellas flitted amongst the branches, squawking and calling. Seagulls dotted the beach, running as a group away from Fudge who tore towards them, tongue lolling, yapping like a mad creature.

"He loves it down here. I feel bad for the seagulls, but he needs the exercise." Bea watched the dog with a grimace.

"At least they can fly out of the way."

Beatrice called Fudge back to her side and tied him up to a small tree. He lay in the shade, panting.

Charmaine put on her mask, snorkel and flippers. She waved hello to Aidan, who sat on the sand beside a large surf-board. There were no waves to speak of, and she doubted he'd be able to do much more than float on the board if he took it out. She waddled to the water's edge and stepped into it. The cold took her breath away at first, but she soon grew used to it and found that the water was warmer than it'd seemed at first.

The reef was as spectacular as she remembered. She spent the next hour swimming slowly around it, revelling in the feel of the water on her skin, the sun on her head, the sight of the coral and the fish who swam so close she could almost reach out and touch them, but when she tried, they were gone before her fingers closed around a fistful of water.

Finally, she dragged herself out of the ocean, reluctant to leave. She could snorkel all day and still not get enough of this place. Bea and Aidan had already waved goodbye and left. There was nothing to show they'd been there other than some indents in the sand where they'd sat together, snug up against one another with the afternoon sun golden on their wet bodies. They'd talked together and laughed, Bea looking up into Aidan's handsome face with a kind of adoration Charmaine had only wished for herself. She'd never been in love, and often wondered if she ever would be. She was awkward and uncomfortable around most people. It made meeting new people difficult for her.

She dried herself off and cycled home, feeling tired and satisfied. When she opened the door and pushed her bike inside, she found Watson curled up in her armchair. She squatted beside the chair and stroked his back. He purred and stretched out so she could scratch beneath his chin and around his ears.

The sight of the cat, completely at home in her flat, warmed her heart. He didn't have anywhere he felt comfortable in the world, and neither did she. But perhaps both of them could make a home together here, the misfit woman and the wandering cat.

"I know you have a home, but I heard about the new dog. If you want, you can stay here with me or visit whenever you like. If the dog gets particularly annoying or it eats your food or something, I'll feed you, and you can steal my armchair. We can be alone together."

The animal purred more loudly, and she squeezed onto the armchair beside him. He made room for her, letting one of his legs dangle across hers. His pink paw flexed, and his eyes blinked shut as she continued stroking his face gently. For the first time in a long time, she was happy.

Eight

EVER SINCE PENNY and Rowan's engagement party, Bea had been troubled by allergies. She sniffled as she padded about the kitchen to make her morning coffee. With a tissue pressed to her nose, she sneezed three times, then blinked back the tears to reach for her cup and carried it into the living room. Usually she'd drink her coffee sitting on the back deck, looking out over her semi-private beach, but not today. With allergies giving her so much grief, she'd chosen to sit indoors and turn the air-conditioning on instead.

If she kept the windows shut, she should manage to get through the day without too much difficulty. It was her day off from the café, and she had nothing to do. She'd promised to spend the day with Aidan, but if he wanted to go bush-walking or swimming, she'd have to turn him down. It wouldn't be very attractive for her to spend the entire day red-eyed, sneezing into a handful of tissues and sniffling all over him. Usually her allergies didn't last long, there must've been a particular tree on the island that flowered at that time.

Things between them were going well. Really well. She couldn't recall a time in her life when she'd felt so peaceful about a relationship. With Preston, she'd always been a little on edge — he didn't like it when she was emotional or needy. She had to make sure everything was just right, since he preferred a tidy house and liked a plan on weekends. But with Aidan, she could be herself. He had no expectations, didn't get upset at her if she reacted emotionally to something. Didn't mind if she spoke throughout the movie. Laughed when she told silly jokes. And happily made Sunday plans for the two of them on her day off without requiring any input from her.

She sipped the coffee while flicking through a magazine that showed images of perfectly styled houses that appeared to have no one actually living in them. Then she got changed into a sundress with large yellow flowers on a midnight background.

When Aidan's truck pulled into her driveway, she met him at the front door with a kiss, then sneezed into a tissue in her hand.

He backed away, eyes widening. "Are you sick?"

"Allergies," she explained with a cough.

"That's no good." He followed her into the cottage, but kept his distance. "Are you sure you want to go out today?"

"I can't," she explained as she filled the espresso machine. "Coffee?"

"I'd love one," he replied, then rubbed her back as she made it. "So, would you still like to do something, or do you want alone time?"

"I was looking forward to spending time with you. But as you can see, I'm not very good company today."

"I don't mind if you don't. I'm sure we can come up with something we can do together."

She handed him a cup of coffee, and the two of them sat at her small kitchen table.

"I'd like that, as long as it doesn't bother you to see me sneezing and weepy all day."

He laughed. "Why would that bother me?"

There were so many things about Preston she'd have to unlearn. Things in her relationship that no longer caused the same kind of angst she'd put up with for decades. Preston would've blamed her for the allergies and insisted she stay away from him until she was feeling better.

"Okay, what do you suggest?"

"Come to my place. I can close everything up and put my air purifier on. You can take an antihistamine. The rest is a surprise. Wear comfy clothes and be prepared to be pampered." His eyes sparkled as he reached for her hand. "I've been waiting all week to see you. I'm not going to miss out because of some pollen."

* * *

By the time Aidan had closed up his house, turned on the air purifier and settled with Bea on the couch in his living room, her sinuses were already feeling better. The medicine helped too. He flicked on the television and handed her a bowl of popcorn. Nelly, his golden retriever, lay at Bea's feet, her tail thumping in satisfaction against the floorboards every now and then when Bea spoke.

"Movie marathon," he said.

She smiled, took a handful of popcorn and passed the bowl back to him. "That's perfect. I've been so busy with work, it's nice to have some time off my feet."

They watched a rom-com, after which she lay on the couch, her stomach full of popcorn and soda water, and sighed at the ceiling.

"I love a good rom-com, but right now, all it's doing is reminding me of Dani's situation."

"What's going on with Dani?" Aidan asked.

"It's her new boyfriend. They're still dating. I'd hoped it

would end quickly, but she seems even more smitten than she was before."

He quirked an eyebrow. "Ah, yes, that's right. The architecture lecturer who uses cushions for furniture. Do you want to talk about it?"

"No, not really. But he's so much older than her. He's a lecturer at the university, and I have to say, the feminist in me isn't happy about the power dynamic there. He's taking advantage of her."

Aidan took her hand and wound his fingers through hers. "But it's her life. She's an adult, and she seems to like him."

"But she doesn't know what's best. She's still so young."

"I know you're worried about her making the same mistakes you did, but perhaps you'll just have to trust her."

"I trust *her*..."

"I know you do. But maybe you should have a conversation with her. Be honest — tell her how you feel, what you're concerned about."

"She'll be so angry," Bea objected, her cheeks warming as anxiety filled her gut.

"You either have to let it go and accept him into her life for now, or you have to speak up and risk her being angry with you."

"Like you said, she's an adult. What if I push her away and she doesn't want to see me anymore? Look at Betsy and her son—they've spent years apart. I stayed away from Coral Island for so long because I didn't want to be around my father and Bradford. She might do the same."

He sighed and kissed Bea on the tip of her nose. "Then maybe you shouldn't say anything."

"But she might marry him."

He laughed. "It seems to me you're in between a rock and a hard place."

She groaned. "I know—that's the problem. I don't know

what to do. Either direction I take, I could make a huge mistake."

"Life's a conundrum," he said. "Should we order some lunch and watch the next movie? Maybe we can solve all the world's problems while we wait."

She sighed. "Yes, that's a good idea. I can't think straight on an empty stomach. "

"How about Thai food?"

They ordered the food and talked about life and their hopes and dreams while they waited for it to be delivered. Bea pushed thoughts of Dani and her situation aside and focused on their conversation instead. When it arrived, the delicious scent of the Thai cuisine made Bea's stomach clench with hunger. They set it all out on the coffee table, on a plain white tablecloth, and sat to eat. Bea's hip was feeling better after she'd taken pain relief and used a heat pack on the affected area the previous day.

She was so hungry, the food tasted better than anything she'd eaten in as long as she could remember. Or maybe it was the company. It was so nice to sit and talk with Aidan as though they were teenagers all over again, but without the hang-ups, insecurities or the pain of loss she'd experienced back then. All those things were behind them now. They were free to be themselves and to love each other with their whole hearts.

She took a large bite of slow-cooked beef massaman with red chillies. The flavours burst across her tongue, leaving a tingling of spices behind. The coconut rice was perfectly cooked, and the Pad Thai light and tasty.

"Have you ever considered living somewhere else? Other than Coral Island?" Aidan asked.

She swallowed. "I didn't think I'd ever end up here, so yes. I really had no plans other than to raise my children. After that, I thought Preston and I might travel while I built up my catering company, but the divorce disrupted all my ideas about how my life would go. Now, my plans have changed and I'm embracing the uncertainty. What about you?"

He shrugged. "I was somewhat the same as you. My goal was to grow old with my wife, but then she got sick and all I could think about was helping her get well—surviving, really. Then she died, and I didn't know what to do with myself. That's why I came back to the island. It was my grounding point. The one place I felt at home in the midst of all the turmoil."

"And now?"

"I was beginning to get back to that place where I could do something ... adventurous, I suppose. But then you came home."

"Then I came home." She smiled. "What kind of adventures?"

"I'd love to travel as well. I never did much of that. When I was playing football, I was stuck in the training schedule, taking care of my physical health, dealing with media interviews and all of that. Then I was looking after my wife."

"Travelling sounds good," Bea said.

"Maybe we should do that together." A smile lit up his face. There was nothing she wanted more than to see the world with Aidan by her side.

"I'd love that."

He shifted closer to her and rested a hand on her knee. "I want to do everything together."

Her heart skipped a beat. "I do too. I can't imagine us being apart."

"There's no reason we should be. Not any longer. Grace is settled back with her mother now, and she'll visit during the school holidays. But other than her and my work, I have no commitments to anyone. Just you."

"I have the café, but it's doing really well now even when

I'm not there. I could find someone to manage it if we wanted to take a trip somewhere."

"Could you?" He quirked an eyebrow. "Because that would probably be all we'd need."

"Definitely," she replied. "I can't wait to see the world with you."

"Where would we go first?"

She bit down on her lower lip. There were so many places she wanted to go, things she longed to see. "Maybe we should go to Italy. It's supposed to be romantic, with so much history and art."

"That would be a great start," he replied. "Let's book a trip."

"That simple?" She laughed. "Surely you should argue with me or something. It's all too easy."

"Why argue? You're absolutely right — Italy is the perfect country for us to start our adventure together. In fact, we could get married there."

Her breath caught in her throat. "What?"

"We should get married while we're in Italy." He raised himself up onto one knee and took her left hand in his. "I want us to get married. I've wanted it for as long as I can remember. We were perfect together when we were younger, but life pulled us apart. Now there's no reason for us to put it off any longer. You're the one, the woman who stole my heart before I even knew what love was. I want to spend the rest of our lives together. Will you marry me?"

Her eyes blurred with tears, and her heart thudded against her rib cage. "Yes, I will."

He pulled her up onto her knees and against his chest. His arms wrapped around her, then one hand cupped her jaw as he leaned down to kiss her. His lips were soft against hers as he explored her mouth, gently at first, then growing with passion as the realisation of what they'd just agreed to hit them both.

Tears wet her cheeks as they kissed, then she laughed against his mouth and pulled away to gaze into his eyes.

"We're getting married?"

He pulled a small box out of the pocket of his shorts and opened it. A large diamond-encrusted blue jewel sparkled under the soft glow of the lamplight. He slipped the ring out of the box and onto her ring finger.

She gaped. "You already bought a ring?"

He grinned. "I've been planning to ask you for a while, but wanted to wait for the perfect moment."

"I can't believe we're getting married," she said, staring at the ring, then wiping the tears from her cheeks with her fingertips.

"It's been a long time coming," he said, kissing her still-damp cheeks.

"And we can spend the rest of our lives making up for that."

Nine

THE ENTIRE SHOP was packed to the brim with flowers. Expected, for a florist shop, but more jammed in than usual. There was barely any room to move, and the scent from the extra bunches of lilies had become so intense that Charmaine had to pop out of the shop every now and then to gasp for breaths of fresh air. The preposterous idea that floral arrangements would be too beautifully scented had never once entered her mind before. But now she understood why so many of their clients asked to hold back on the lilies when they put together an arrangement for a special occasion.

Betsy had rushed from appointment to appointment all morning long. But now it was midday, and she was seated at the small desk in the back of the shop doing paperwork while eating a sandwich. There was a crease of concentration across her forehead, and one foot tapped incessantly on the floor. Her long silk kaftan was purple with orange and yellow flowers, and she had a matching ribbon tied neatly around her grey curls. Purple eyeshadow coated both eyelids, and she had red lipstick smudged around one side of her mouth while perfectly applied on the other. She glanced in the mirror hanging behind the desk and fixed her lipstick before taking another bite of sandwich.

Charmaine set a stack of flyers advertising their wedding arrangements on the table in the centre of the room and studied her a moment. She was curious to ask Betsy how she was doing, but didn't want to intrude or step over the line. In recent weeks her son had yelled at her, then she'd gotten into a disagreement with Penny's mother at the engagement party. Yet she always appeared completely unruffled. It was difficult for Charmaine to figure out whether it was appropriate to ask her boss personal questions. But Betsy had been so good to her in the weeks since she started working there, she honestly cared.

"Betsy, do you mind if I interrupt to ask you a question?"

Betsy paused, put down her pen and looked at Charmaine with curiosity in her tired eyes. "Not at all, honey. Shoot."

"There's a cat called Watson who showed up at my back door. I let him into the flat, and he seems to have made himself at home there. I thought I should talk to you about it and make sure you don't mind."

Betsy waved a hand. "Not at all. Watson's more like a neighbourhood cat than anything. I'm glad he's comfortable around you. He never seems to want to spend any time with me, even though I've often left him a saucer of milk by the back door. I guess he's particular about who he befriends." She chuckled.

Charmaine smiled. "Thank you — I'm sure he won't leave a mess or anything. And I'll clean up after him if he does." It seemed everyone in town knew Watson. They all had the same story — he was a community cat, but didn't take to people easily. She was grateful he'd chosen her. He was already a big part of her life. She only hoped he'd stick around.

"It's fine, honey. I trust you to take care of things."

Charmaine linked her hands together behind her back.

"Betsy, I was just wondering... You can tell me if I'm being too nosy, but... If it's not too much of an imposition, are you okay?"

Betsy swallowed a bite of sandwich and peered at her over half-moon glasses perched on her thin nose. "I'm fine, honey. Why do you ask?"

"The other day, I saw you in here throwing papers around. It seemed as though you were a bit frazzled. And another time, your son was shouting... Anyway, it's really none of my business. But if there's anything I can do to help..."

Betsy smiled. "Well, aren't you a darling. Thank you, honey. I really appreciate it. And yes, I suppose I'm having a bit of a rough time lately. I don't mind you asking one little bit. It's nice to have friends who care."

She hadn't thought of herself as Betsy's friend before, but the idea was an appealing one since she didn't have many friends. She'd left her last friend behind when she fled her home after her mother's death. And since then, she'd barely stayed in one place long enough to build any kind of meaningful relationship.

"You're welcome," she said, unsure how else to respond. She twisted the hem of her shirt around, looking for more words to say but finding her mind blank.

Betsy shuffled over to where Charmaine stood. "The truth is, my brother is in prison."

Charmaine's mouth fell open. "In prison? For what?" she said without thinking.

Betsy sighed. "Some people think he killed a woman a long time ago. But he didn't—he's innocent. They proved him innocent back then, so I don't know why we have to go through this all over again. It seems entirely unfair to me."

"Wow," Charmaine said, regretting her thoughtless question. Mum had always admonished her about her impulsive words.

Think about other people's feelings. Soften your sentences, she'd say.

"I'm so sorry to hear that," Charmaine replied, her words gentler. "That must be very hard for you."

"The worst of it is, he'd finally pulled his life back together and was living quietly, alone. He didn't hurt anyone—didn't do anything to deserve this. It seems so wrong. But it is what it is, I suppose." She blinked. "Anyway, I was looking for some coins. I had a collection, you see. A long time ago. I put them together, in case of hard times. And now I can't for the life of me remember where I stowed them. Somewhere safe, of course. I was going to use them to pay for his lawyer—they call them solicitors over here. I went through everything in this entire room and didn't see a sign of them. You haven't seen any old coins lying around, have you? They're quite valuable."

Charmaine shook her head. "No, but if I do, I'll be sure to let you know."

It was prescience, or destiny, or something like that — it had to be. Both of them had been through so much with their families. Both had wayward brothers. Of course, the difference was that Charmaine's brother was missing and she had no idea where to find him. Whether he was innocent of the things she suspected him of doing was another thing. Maybe he'd end up in prison himself one day. She hoped she was wrong about that — she loved him still, regardless of the way he'd treated her after their mother's death. And perhaps he had a good reason for disappearing and leaving her to cope with it all alone. She didn't know because he hadn't contacted her. Not once.

Thinking about it now, it seemed even stranger than it had before. Perhaps he was hurt, or in trouble. She hadn't considered that before, although why not, she couldn't say. She thought of him as indestructible — her big, strong, older brother. Nothing could touch him. He was charismatic, fearless, loveable and endlessly frustrating all at once. If only he would let her know that he was okay and where he was staying, it would give her peace of mind. But he either hadn't thought it necessary to do that, or he was unable to. Maybe she should contact the police and report him missing. But what if he was on the run?

If Betsy's brother was wrongfully imprisoned, she felt bad for him and for Betsy. It would be difficult to live your entire life under the shadow of guilt for a crime you didn't commit. No wonder Betsy seemed on edge sometimes.

"I have to help him raise bail, if he's allowed it when he goes to his hearing tomorrow. But I can't seem to pull the money together. I guess I'll figure it out somehow. Maybe I'll put a mortgage on the shop."

"Oh, surely you won't have to do that."

Betsy shrugged, then returned to her desk. "Don't you worry yourself about it, Chaz, my girl. I'll work on something and figure it out. I always do. The trial will happen in a few months, and hopefully life can go back to normal after that."

"It must be very stressful for you," Charmaine said.

Betsy nodded as she took a seat at her desk. "It's hard to believe we're going through all this again. For so many years, there were rumours on the island, people talking behind their hands whenever we were around. Didn't believe he was innocent. But lately, it'd been better. People forgot all about it. Until some supposed evidence came to light a few months ago."

"Evidence?"

"Oh, it was nothing, really. It doesn't prove anything at all. But the police wanted to be diligent. They caught a lot of flak during the original investigation. People thought they botched it. And they did—they spent far too much time chasing up rumours about my brother instead of looking for the real killer. And now we're going to face it all again. Sometimes I wonder..."

"What do you wonder?"

Betsy ran a hand over her eyes. "Nothing, really. I couldn't leave the island. Not with my family still here. But it's hard to stay."

"And your business, of course."

"That too." She smiled. "I'm grateful for you, honey. You coming along when you did really saved me. I can't tell you how much you being here makes a difference."

"I'm glad I can help."

Betsy shot her a warm smile. There were tears in her eyes. "It means a lot." She inhaled a quick breath. "I'm surprised you didn't see the story about Buck on the news when they arrested him. It was aired around the country."

Charmaine thought back to the last few times she'd watched the news and couldn't recall anything like what Betsy was referring to. "I don't watch the news often. In fact, I've given up on most screens these days — phone, TV, computer. I use them for work, but otherwise, I don't really spend time in the digital world."

Betsy frowned. "Well now, that's unusual for your generation."

"I suppose so. But after my mother died, I found I was spending far too much time on screens. I left my hometown and all my friends behind, and so I did all my interacting online. In the end, I found it made me anxious and irritable. I felt more alone than ever. So, I decided to give it up. I've hardly been online since other than to look for maps and things like that."

"Good for you. That's how life used to be, and we turned out all right. Didn't we?" Betsy grinned. "Do you have any siblings?"

How much should she say? Betsy had been so good to her,

had been vulnerable and shared about her own life and trials. But Charmaine generally didn't open up to people. It wasn't something she was comfortable doing. She hesitated, then spoke gingerly.

"I have a brother too."

"Where is he? Are the two of you close?"

"We were close when we were young," Charmaine replied. "But we've lost contact."

"Oh, that's too bad," Betsy said with a shake of her head. "I'm sorry to hear that. Family is so important. I know how painful it can be when you're not able to see them or speak to them as often as you'd like. My son and I had a falling out, you see. It was years ago now, but we're doing what we can to mend fences. And I'm grateful for every chance, even if it does mean we fight sometimes."

That explained the shouting, Charmaine thought. It made sense that there'd be tension if the two of them were working to rebuild a broken relationship. "Good on you. Family relationships can be tough."

Betsy grinned. "Now ain't that the truth."

"I should be looking for him, I suppose. He's the only family connection I have left. But I want to be here, on the island, ignoring the rest of the world and my family problems. Life on the mainland can go on without me, and instead of being part of it, I can spend the day snorkelling in paradise and avoiding it all."

"Sounds like a perfect plan," Betsy said, although her voice was low and soft. "There are certainly no rules about having to put ourselves through the torture of chasing after our loved ones. Well done to you for recognising that fact and moving on with your life. Now, where are we on the St James wedding? Oh, wait! I figured it out!" Betsy leaped to her feet and shuffled from the room. She returned with a large black folder that she set on the table with a grunt. She flicked it open, and rows of coins gleamed from within slotted pages.

She laughed out loud. "I knew I'd remember. They were in the floor safe."

"Floor safe?"

Betsy waved her off. "Never mind. Obviously I don't use it. I haven't looked in that thing in years. That's why I forgot where the coins were. But now that I have them, I can sell some of them to pay for Buck's bail."

Charmaine couldn't help feeling happy for Betsy, but at the same time, she wondered whether Betsy was right about her brother or if she was about to set a murderer free to roam around Coral Island.

Ten

THE TAWNY FROGMOUTH'S wing was bent at an odd angle. Penny held the bird steady on the table as the vet fixed it and wound a bandage around its body.

"You have any plans for the weekend?"

"Wedding preparations. We've got to plan our honeymoon as well," Penny replied with a sigh. "Any suggestions?"

"Cairns is nice, or Port Douglas."

"We have such lovely beaches here on Coral Island, I'd probably prefer to go somewhere really different. Rowan travels all the time, but I've hardly been anywhere."

"Then you should try New Zealand. It's close, but it's very different to what you're used to. And it's stunningly beautiful."

She chewed the inside of her cheek. It was a good suggestion. Perhaps she should talk to Rowan about it. He'd said she could choose where they went, since he'd already been everywhere. He'd finished up the last of his contracted stories and wasn't taking on any more now that they'd decided he should work with her at the refuge. It'd been three days so far, and already she was relaxing into their new partnership. It was going better than she'd thought it would.

"Thanks for the recommendation. I'll take a look at it. But honestly, it'll be so nice to get away, just the two of us, that I'm not very fussed about where we go. I'm looking forward to having that time together. I can't believe I'm finally getting married." Nerves stirred in the pit of her gut.

Karen, the vet, smiled at her over the top of the bird's raised head. "I know... I never thought I'd see the day that Penny St James would tie the knot."

She swallowed. "It's exciting and a little scary."

"Piece of cake." Karen winked. "You're going to love it."

"You like being married, right?"

"It can be wonderful and hard all at the same time. I wouldn't give it up, though."

"Everyone says it takes work, and I've been in long-term relationships before, so I get it. We never walked down the aisle, but I've had my fair share of conflicts. I even went to couples' counselling with one old boyfriend. I thought we'd get married, but in the end, we weren't right for one another. I can't imagine being married to him now."

"I know what you mean," Karen said as she packed up her things. "I hate to think how my life would be if I'd married that sailor from Seattle years ago. Some things aren't meant to be."

The idea of getting married was a little overwhelming for Penny. But whenever she pictured Rowan's smiling face and his hand holding hers, she knew they'd made the right decision. Whatever the future held, they'd face it together, and she was certain they'd be able to make it through.

* * *

When Karen left the refuge, Penny went looking for Rowan. He was in the small office behind the snake enclosure, staring at a computer screen. He tapped on the keyboard, then his gaze drifted up to meet hers and his mouth broke into a wide grin.

"Are you almost finished?" she asked, walking over to sit in his lap.

He kissed her and wrapped his arms around her waist. "Just about. You?"

"I'm done for the day. It feels good to be able to say that. Thanks to you, I don't have to take home a pile of paperwork to do after dinner."

He arched an eyebrow. "That's good news. It means more time and attention for me."

She laughed and pried herself free. "Finish your work, and we can leave. I've got some fish in the fridge. I thought I'd make you a curry."

"I love fish curry."

"I know you do," she quipped. "I'll meet you at the beach house. I've got to talk to Charmaine one last time about our wedding plans."

"I'll see you there, then," he said with a wave.

She stood at the door, leaning against the frame, watching him as he got back to work. Her heart thundered against her rib cage. Had they made the right decision? She loved that his being there took the load off her shoulders, but what about him? He was used to travelling the globe, chasing down stories and publishing them for all the world to read. Now he was filling out boring paperwork at a small animal sanctuary.

"Are you sure you're going to be fulfilled working here?"

He glanced up at her, eyes narrowed. "Huh?"

"You gave up a pretty glamorous career to move back to Coral Island and work a menial administrative job." She shrugged. "I don't want you to equate boring admin work with being married to me."

He laughed. "Okay, I promise not to do that."

She chewed on her lip. "I hear you saying it, but I'm not sure it's really convincing."

"What do you want me to do? How can I reassure you?"

"I don't know." She wandered back to his desk and perched on the edge of it. "Do you think you'll miss your career?"

"Probably," he admitted.

Her eyes widened. "What?"

"It's fine, though. Of course there'll be things about it that I'll miss. But I won't miss having to live out of hotel rooms, or chase down leads, or push a microphone into grieving people's faces. There are plenty of aspects to the job that I'm glad to give up."

"Because you don't have to do it... You don't have to give it up for me."

"I know that." He looped an arm around her and pulled her close. "I want to. I need a break. It's not just about you— this is a chance for me to do something different with my life. And who knows? Maybe I'll go back to it one day. But for now, it's time for me to go in another direction."

There was a knock at the office door, and Charmaine poked her head inside. "Penny?"

Penny hurried to meet her. "I'm in here."

"I hope I'm not interrupting you two lovebirds," Charmaine said with a shy smile.

Penny laughed. "Not at all. Come with me. We can talk in my office." She blew Rowan a kiss and led Charmaine down the hall to her private office. It was small and cramped, with filing cabinets lining the walls and photographs of her with a variety of animals in mismatched frames hung above the cabinets.

Charmaine's large grey eyes swept around the room, taking it in. "I love seeing the way you take care of these animals. You're a hero to them, you know?"

Penny's face warmed. "I don't know about that."

"Definitely a superhero."

"That's very kind of you. I love them, so I do what I can to help them. It's the best job in the world."

"You're lucky. I haven't really found work that I'm so passionate about. Although I'm beginning to enjoy arranging flowers and wedding planning."

Penny sat at her desk and indicated for Charmaine to sit across from her. "What other types of work have you done?"

"When I left school, I didn't know what to do, so I worked in retail for a couple of years. But then I discovered archaeology, and I decided to give it a try at university. It was great, but in the end, not for me."

"What happened?" Penny leaned back in her chair.

"My mother died. After that, I couldn't really concentrate on my studies anymore."

"I'm sorry to hear that," Penny said. "That must've been hard."

"She was my family. I don't have anyone else—no one who cares enough to stick around, anyway. So, after she died, I quit university, sold up everything I owned and left town."

"Which town was that?"

"Newcastle."

"Do you miss it?"

"It's been a few years since I left. I'm twenty-five now. But I think about it every now and then. The memories are getting less sad with each year that passes. Maybe one day I'll go back —I don't know. I like it here now."

"Coral Island will definitely grow on you," Penny admitted.

"I remember you saying you've spent your whole life here — did you ever leave?"

"I had a few years on the mainland, studying zoology."

"I'm hoping to make this my home. I like the way it feels, and everyone is so kind to each other. The other day, I was carrying my groceries down the street, and a man I've never met before offered to help me with them. I couldn't believe it."

Penny nodded. "It's that kind of place. I love it here too. We all look after each other, although there are plenty of secrets. Still, that's part of its charm, I suppose."

"We should go through all of your wedding selections," Charmaine said, changing tack suddenly as she drew a loose-leaf folder out of her shoulder bag. "We're getting close to the big day, and I want to make sure I've got everything just right for you."

Footsteps thudded down the corridor, and Beatrice hurried in with a quick knock on her way through the door. "I was hoping I'd find you. Oh, hello, Chaz. It's good to see you."

"Bea, what's going on?" Penny caught her friend with both hands as she barrelled around the desk.

Bea puffed lightly. She drew a deep breath. "I came from the courthouse. The magistrate has released Buck on bail. He's out."

Eleven

THE NUMBER on the phone screen was as familiar to her as Vegemite on toast. It was her mother's mobile phone number, and she'd paid the bill every month for the past three years ever since Mum died. She couldn't bring herself to let it go until she moved to Coral Island.

It'd been one of the decisions she made when she settled on the island — to finally stop paying the fee for the phone and give up the chance to call it to listen to her mother's voicemail message one last time. If she didn't give it up, she'd be paying that bill for the rest of her life. The more time that passed, the more difficult it became. She had to move on. There was no therapist in her life, no counsellor to tell her the best way to move forward, but she knew that much. Letting go was the first step.

Still, it'd been harder than she'd thought it would be. She held her phone up, dialled the number and let it ring. The line rang out with the ear-piercing chime that announced the number had been disconnected. She hung it up as tears pooled in the corners of her eyes, then slid silently down her cheeks.

What now?

She'd let go. She'd moved on and found a place to settle, to start over. What should she do next? She had a job she enjoyed, had made a few acquaintances, had a cat (kind of) and a life (sort of). There ought to be some element of satisfaction — as though she'd achieved something great. Instead, she only felt empty inside. She was still alone in the world and didn't know what to do with her life or how to move on with no family or close friends.

The world was a lonely place.

If only she'd asked more questions about the extended family, but her mother had been so reluctant to open up that Charmaine had left it alone. She didn't know much about aunts, uncles, cousins or grandparents. Only that her grandparents were gone — she assumed that meant dead, but now, looking back, she realised it could've meant anything really. Her mother didn't talk about her family often, so Charmaine had believed her to be an only child for many years.

If only she'd said more about her sister, given Charmaine further hints about the woman or how to get in contact with her, that would've been something. But she'd done a search on her mother's maiden name and hadn't found anything useful. It was a common name and there'd been hundreds of results — how could she find an aunt who'd very likely changed her name after getting married and she had no recollection of ever meeting?

Watson wandered across the floor, then collapsed onto his side in the middle of the living room with strange, stilted movements. Charmaine cocked her head to one side. He'd been more lethargic than usual for the past few days and had barely eaten the food she'd set out for him. Perhaps he was ill. She placed her phone on the couch and went to sit by his side.

"What's wrong, buddy?"

He didn't seem to be able to walk properly when he stood again. The animal opened his mouth, and a pitiful meow came out. She picked him up gingerly and stroked his head. His breathing was laboured. Something was wrong with him. She should take him to the vet. A quick search on her phone found that there was a vet's office on the other side of Kellyville. It looked to be open, but it was several kilometres from her flat and she couldn't ride her bike and take care of the cat, so she'd have to walk.

She scooped Watson into her arms and carried him down the steps and out through the front of the florist shop, stopping to lock it behind her awkwardly. Then she set off along the Main Street. When she reached the corner, she almost ran into Beatrice Rushton, who wasn't looking where she was going, her gaze fixed across the street on the primary school when she stepped out of her café.

"Excuse me. Sorry!" Charmaine cried as she stumbled and caught herself by grabbing hold of Bea's arm.

"Are you okay?" Bea asked, grabbing Charmaine with both hands and setting her right. "I wasn't paying attention."

"It's fine," Charmaine replied. "I'm in a hurry, so it was my fault."

"What's wrong?" Bea asked, studying the cat with concern.

"I think Watson's sick. I'm not sure what's going on with him, but he's a little confused and walking strangely."

"The vet's a long way from here. Why don't I drive you?" Bea suggested.

Charmaine gratefully accepted the offer, and they hurried to Bea's old station wagon. On the way, Charmaine noticed Evie waving to them from inside the bookshop. She stepped outside, a frown on her face.

"What's going on?"

"We're headed to the vet. Something's wrong with Watson," Bea explained.

"I'll drive you," Evie said. "My car is faster."

"There's nothing wrong with my station wagon," Bea objected as the three of them scurried down the street to where Evie's sports car was parked.

"Of course there's not, honey," Evie said. "I'm sure you'd have gotten her to the vet eventually."

Bea huffed. "Perhaps we should race there."

"No racing, please," Charmaine begged. "I really want to get to the vet in one piece."

"You're right. Bea, this isn't the time. Maybe later we can test out your theory on the drive to the inn." Evie winked at Bea, who laughed.

They reached the blue sports car, and Evie opened the passenger door and slid the seat forwards for Bea, who climbed inelegantly into the back. Then she slid the seat back for Charmaine, who settled inside, being careful not to jostle Watson as much as she could manage. Evie jogged around to the driver's side and joined them.

Once they were inside the car, the trip was a short one, and Charmaine soon had the cat safely handed off to the vet, who rushed him into an examination room. Charmaine followed while Bea and Evie stayed behind in the waiting room.

The vet examined the cat, who by that time was panting. "Did he eat anything unusual," he asked.

Charmaine thought for a moment. "There was a piece of chocolate on the coffee table. I didn't think to check if it was gone, I'm sorry."

"What kind of chocolate?"

"Dark chocolate with almonds. It's my favourite."

He smiled. "Chocolate is toxic for cats. They don't often partake, but if he ate even a little bit of it, he could get very sick. I'm going to induce vomiting and give him some charcoal," he announced. "If he didn't eat too much, he should recover within a few hours."

Charmaine sighed with relief. "He's going to be okay?"

"We'll know for sure in three to five hours, but he looks healthy and strong. I don't see why he wouldn't recover. It's good you brought him in now, though. If you'd waited, we might've had a different result."

She joined Bea and Evie in the waiting room while Watson underwent his treatment, and slumped into a chair beside them.

"Any updates?" Evie asked cautiously.

"We think he ate chocolate. But the vet says he's going to be fine."

"Phew," Bea said, resting a hand on Charmaine's arm. "That was a little stressful. I remember taking Fudge to the vet once when he was a puppy and he ate some chocolate he found stashed under Harry's bed. It's a horrible feeling."

"I didn't even think about it — I'll have to be more careful with where I leave food in the future." Charmaine shook her head, throat aching.

Now that her adrenaline had abated, she felt as though she might cry. She straightened in her seat and drew a long, deep breath. She hated displaying her emotions publicly and did whatever she could to keep them to herself. Even though Watson was a cat, and not *her* cat, she'd already grown attached to him. Besides that, he was really the only family she had now — something which she knew was a reflection on how utterly pathetic her life had become, but which she couldn't do a single thing about.

The fact that these two women had not only shown her sympathy but had fought over who could get her to the vet faster, then waited patiently for her to emerge from the examination room, only made her more emotional.

"Thank you," she said with a sniffle.

"You're welcome," Evie replied.

"I'm glad he's going to be okay. I know how much our

pets can mean to us." Bea's eyebrows drew together in concern.

"I know he's only a neighbourhood cat, not really mine. But we spend a lot of time together..." She wiped her nose with a tissue she pulled from her purse.

"No need to explain. We completely understand." Bea waved a hand.

"I can't tell you how much it means to me that you both cared enough to come." She swallowed around a lump in her throat. "It's been a long time since I had friends who would do something like that."

Bea reached for her hand and squeezed it, her eyes glimmering. "I don't know much about your former life. Isn't there anyone back home you can call on?"

Charmaine shook her head and wiped her nose again. "No."

"What about family?" Evie asked.

"My mother died, my brother is missing... It's just me."

Both women's eyes widened in surprise. It was the same thing when she told anyone snippets of her history. They were shocked by the idea of a missing brother and saddened by her predicament. She hated the pitying looks—that was why she rarely spoke up or opened her heart to new people. But these women were different. They'd reached out to her before they knew anything about her. She felt as though she could trust them with the little pieces of herself that remained after so much had been ripped apart.

"Well, you can always give me a call if you need anything," Bea said matter-of-factly.

"Me as well," Evie added with a quick nod of her head, making her red curls bounce. "Anything at all. You let me know."

"Thanks. I appreciate that." Charmaine's throat ached. "I wanted so badly to call my mother this morning, but I finally took the step to disconnect her phone. So, I was having a bit of a pity party for myself when I noticed Watson walking funny."

Bea and Evie exchanged a pointed look.

Bea offered Charmaine a wide smile. "When you're ready to go home, we'll all head to the café and have iced coffees with the biggest piece of caramel chocolate cake you've ever seen in your life."

Charmaine grinned through the tears. "I'd like that."

Twelve

THE NEWS FLASHED across the television screen, and Penny stood watching with arms folded. She still couldn't believe it'd happened — Buck Clements had been out of prison on bail for two days, and a contingent of press had followed his progress across to the island. Everyone was doing their best to stay out of the way. Penny had no desire to be caught up in a paparazzi frenzy, but the police officer she'd spoken to assured her that the media was likely to go home within days and not to worry.

"Just keep your head down," he'd said.

And she'd done exactly that. Rowan had apologised for the behaviour of his fellow journalists, although from her perspective, they weren't the problem. It was Buck — he was the one accused of murder, and for some reason their justice system had felt compelled to set him free before his trial.

Were they supposed to let murderers out on the street like that? Surely there were rules against things that put the public in danger that way. But she'd never studied the law and she couldn't be certain. All she knew was, it seemed very wrong.

If he killed someone else while he was out, then they'd

really be sorry. She heard about cases like it all the time on the news — someone suspected of murder was let out on bail and went on a killing rampage. She only hoped this time it would be different — after all, as far as any of them knew, Buck hadn't killed anyone *since* her grandmother. At least, not on the island. If there'd been a spate of murders, she'd certainly have heard about it. The community was too small to hide something like that.

"What are you watching?" Rowan wandered in from the kitchen, eating a burrito over a plate. He set the plate on the coffee table and put the burrito on it, then moved to embrace her. "You look particularly ravishing today."

She laughed and ran fingers through her wild blonde curls. "You're just saying that."

"No, I really mean it. Every day that passes, you get more beautiful."

"That's not physically possible."

"And yet it's true." He winked and kissed her. She swooned inside but didn't want to let him know her knees were weak. Sometimes he was just a little too full of himself and utterly aware of his own charms and how they made her feel.

"They let Buck out on bail."

He frowned. "I know." He spun to watch the rest of the news story.

A police officer was being interviewed. The man's dark monobrow poked out beneath his cap. "We're still compiling our case against the defendant. If you have any information about the murder of Mary Brown forty-six years ago, please contact the Coral Island Police Department. We need the help of the entire community to piece together what happened. As I'm sure you can appreciate, the crime was committed so long ago that much of the trail has gone cold. If anyone has information they haven't submitted previously, please step forward.

It could mean the difference between putting a murderer away for the rest of his life or having him return to the community."

Penny shivered in Rowan's arms. "Did you hear that? What do you think it means? You're the journalist—you're used to the way police officers speak about crimes and criminals."

Rowan sighed. "Sounds like they don't have an airtight case."

Her heart clenched. She had been afraid of that. "What if he never gets convicted?"

"Then we'll both have to live with the fact that the only father figure either of us has ever known could be a murderer, but will get away with it and be living on the island as our neighbour."

* * *

Later when Penny drove to the Blue Shoal Inn to meet her friends for lunch, she could hardly think about anything else other than Buck Clements and his freedom. She pulled her car into the lot beside the inn and stepped out to survey the building. She hadn't been to see it since Taya had renovated the place and then sold it to her father's business, *Paradise Resorts*. It looked better than it had in all the time Penny had known it.

The paintwork sparkled white beneath the glare of the sunlight. Black trim and a charcoal-coloured roof accentuated the white walls, and the gardens were meticulously groomed. Everything gleamed brand new, but with the same vintage feel as it'd had before.

She and Rowan had decided to get married on the beach and have their reception at the inn. They wanted to feel the sand beneath their feet while they said their vows. Living on the island for most of their lives, they both felt a connection to the place, as though it should be part of their wedding day. It was something they'd both agreed was important.

She strode inside and found her way to the private dining room where they always met for lunch. The other ladies were already there. She kissed each of their cheeks and collapsed into a chair with a sigh.

"Long day?" Bea asked.

Penny nodded. "The longest. I've already dealt with four hourly feeds for a joey, a five-kilometre run along the beach, two sick animals at the refuge and the news."

Evie sighed. "I saw it too. I knew he was out, since Bea told us all. But seeing it on the television made it so real."

"It gave me the creeps, seeing him like that," Taya said. "To think, we all believed he was innocent. And he was so lovely, giving us cups of tea and chatting about his petunias as though he'd never done a thing wrong in his life. I am embarrassed to admit I thought the gossip about him must've been misleading."

"No, I felt the same way," Penny admitted. "And it was my mother and grandmother he committed the crimes against."

"How does everyone feel about Betsy?" Evie asked. "I mean, we all know she was the one who posted his bail. And she's his alibi. Doesn't it feel strange to run into her around town?"

The other women all exchanged looks. Penny didn't know what to think about the kind little old lady she'd gotten to know better ever since her granddaughter, Sam, had showed up at the animal sanctuary one day and Penny had taken her in and fed her. Now Sam was being cared for each day after school by Betsy, and the little girl's life had completely turned around. She was no longer dirty and neglected, hungry and alone. She had someone to help her, someone to share her life with. Her own father hadn't been able to keep up with everything, since he was single and worked long hours on the mainland to pay the bills. But now Sam had Betsy, and from what Penny could tell, the little girl was happy and well cared for.

"I think we can keep our feelings about Buck separate from our relationship with Betsy," she said.

Bea shrugged. "She comes into the café all the time, and I don't know what to say to her. She's lying for her brother—at least, it seems that way to me. I'm sure he's guilty, but she's giving him an alibi so he gets away with it."

"Has any of you questioned Betsy about his name change?" Taya asked.

Bea shook her head. "I found that driver's license with his picture and a different name in the cave near my cottage, but I never asked her about it."

"Perhaps you should," Evie said.

"You're right, I probably should. I'm not sure how to raise the subject. It's awkward — she's our friend, and I hate to upset her. What do you think about him being so close by?" Bea asked with a shiver as she reached for a glass of chardonnay. "He's just down the road from the inn."

"I'll be locking my doors at night," Taya said. "I've never felt the need before now."

"In fairness, he's always lived a short drive down the road from you, and you've never locked your doors before now," Penny pointed out. She didn't know why she was defending him. She had no reason to. It was her family he'd wronged. But at the same time, he was family too. The web woven around her family and this crime was so complicated, it made her head ache to think about it.

"True, and I don't think he's hurt anyone else."

"It was a crime of passion," Evie offered. "He might not ever hurt anyone again. But that doesn't mean he shouldn't pay for his previous crimes."

"You're right, of course," Penny replied. "But I can't help wondering if maybe we've gotten it wrong. As you said, he hasn't harmed another person, and the police cleared him all those years ago."

"Do you really believe that?" Bea asked, eyes wide. "We found evidence — I found evidence in that cave. Don't you remember? He had the license with a different name on it."

"There could be a million different explanations for that," Penny countered, her chin raised. She shouldn't defend him. But she'd longed to know her father all her life and if this was him, she couldn't believe he would be the type of man who would kill.

Beatrice shifted uncomfortably in her seat. "Perhaps we should talk about something else?"

Evie's nostrils flared.

Taya cleared her throat. "Great idea. In the spirit of changing topics, I got the job."

Everyone's eyes flicked to her face.

Bea grinned. "That's great news!"

"We all knew you'd get it," Evie said as she clapped her hands together.

"Well, I did have the inside track. I know the boss pretty well."

"And you're dating the manager," Penny quipped.

Taya laughed. "That's right — I forgot about that. I'm the boss's daughter *and* the manager's girlfriend. I was a shoo-in. I only feel bad for all the other applicants. Thankfully there weren't any who were remotely qualified, at least according to my father."

"Well, you're going to be fantastic in the role. And you're completely overqualified. I'm so happy for you," Bea said.

Waiters swanned into the dining room with the first trays of food. There were plates of tacos and enchiladas, along with nachos and salads.

"Mexican today," Taya said. "We're testing out some new recipes."

"You're still involved in managing the place?" Penny asked as she spooned a steaming hot enchilada onto her plate.

"Only at a high level. I don't deal with the day-to-day, but I was involved in the overhaul of the menu, training for the manager—those kinds of things."

"So, tell us about the new job." Bea took a bite of nachos.

Penny bit into her enchilada and burned her tongue. She reached for her wine glass and took a mouthful of cold wine. It soothed the burn.

Taya chewed and swallowed a bite of burrito, then dabbed her face with a napkin. "I'll be travelling a lot. I'm going to start in Suva, the capital of Fiji."

"Fiji is beautiful, or so I've heard," Evie said. "You're lucky you'll get to visit places like that."

"I'm looking forward to it. It's going to be a whole new experience for me."

"All those years, you were so busy managing this place, keeping the doors open, raising Camden. You were a good mum and a successful inn owner. You deserve this."

"Thank you," Taya said, eyes gleaming.

Penny raised her wine glass towards Taya, and Taya lifted her own and clinked it against Penny's. Penny spoke up. "Here's to you, Taya, and your new adventure. May it be even better than the last and involve lots of relaxation as well as the challenges you'll no doubt face, and plenty of romance."

They all cheered and raised their glasses to drink.

Taya wiped her eyes. "How did I find such wonderful friends? Thank you."

They ate and talked together for the next hour before Evie finally asked Penny how her wedding preparations were coming.

"It's only two weeks until the wedding, and there's still so much to do," Penny said, feeling her heart rate spike as the words left her lips.

Bea reached out a hand to rest on Penny's shoulder. "You'll be fine. It will all come together, and even if something goes wrong, it will still be fine. It's only one day. Marriage is for life. Well, for some people it is, anyway." She chuckled to herself as she took another bite of food.

Penny chewed on her lower lip. "You're not helping, Bea."

Bea raised both hands. "Yes, come to think of it, you probably need reassurances from someone else — someone who's had a successful marriage."

"Mine didn't last long, although that wasn't because it failed," Taya said. "Not sure I can be of much help."

"And I've never been married," Evie added. "Sorry, no wise words from me. Although I will say this — you always conquer everything you do, Penny. This will be no different. And besides that, I imagine you're looking forward to the honeymoon more than you are the wedding day, since you've never been one to go for stereotypes or tradition."

"That's true," Penny replied. "Thanks—you're all right. It's going to be okay. I've got to stop putting so much pressure on myself to make everything perfect."

"How is Rowan feeling about it all?" Bea asked.

Penny shrugged. "He's so cool and calm about everything. As far as I know, he's perfectly fine. He doesn't seem nervous. He's happy and teases me just as much as usual."

"That's a good sign," Bea said. "Stressful situations bring out the worst in us all. For some people, that's a really bad thing. For others, it shows you that they're able to manage without turning into a crazy person. It sounds like Rowan is even more perfect than he seems."

"Well, he's certainly used to dealing with stress. His job with its deadlines and flights all over the world, the pressure to get it right, threats of losing bylines and so on, seems to have prepared him for this exact moment."

"You mean the wedding, or life with you?" Evie asked, one eyebrow arched.

"Exactly," Penny replied, stabbing a fork in the air.

They all laughed together. Penny joined them, feeling the tension in her shoulders releasing. It was good to spend time with her friends and even better to laugh with them. It helped her keep things in perspective, which was something she desperately needed in that moment with everything that was going on in her life.

"And the best part of all, we've been working together at the animal refuge for a few days now, and we're getting along better than we ever have." Her heart swelled as she recalled the previous day when Rowan had come to her rescue. She'd been inundated with calls and paperwork, and he'd taken it all from her, shooed her outside, and told her to take care of the animals—he'd deal with everything else. She had never felt so relieved.

"You're truly becoming partners. It's a wonderful thing to witness," Taya said with a tear in her eye.

"You're going to make me cry. Stop it," Evie added, reaching for her napkin to pat her cheeks dry.

"You might want to keep that napkin handy," Bea said suddenly. "I've got some news myself."

They all sat in silence, waiting. Penny held her breath.

"Aidan proposed, and I said yes. We're getting married too!"

They all embraced and congratulate her. Penny's heart felt as though it might burst with happiness. She was getting married to the man of her dreams, and now Beatrice would marry the boy she'd fallen in love with when they were still children. They hadn't started dating until Bea and Aidan were sixteen, but Penny clearly remembered them all playing together as friends when they were in primary school. Even back then, Aidan Whitlock had only had eyes for Beatrice.

And now, after all this time, they were finally getting married. She could hardly contain her joy for her lifelong friend. She kissed Bea's cheek, her eyes overflowing.

"I'm so happy for you. Who could've imagined this is where we'd all end up so many years after we met in the Coral Island State School playground?"

Bea wiped her eyes with her fingertips and laughed. "Definitely not me. I wouldn't have believed it two years ago. But here we are."

"If you need someone to help you plan the wedding, Charmaine has been a big help to me. I highly recommend her."

Bea nodded. "Thanks. I think I'll give her call. I have so much on my plate, I don't think I could handle pulling together a wedding on my own. Besides, I've already been married once. This time, I want to do something simple. It's not about the day, but the life lived after it."

"Wise words to remember," Penny said, raising her glass. They all toasted again, then got back to the food. Penny ate in silence, watching each of her friends as they discussed the upcoming weddings and what type of dress Bea would wear, who they'd bring as dates and more. And her heart was full.

Thirteen

STYLISH CONDOS LINED the hillsides of Airlie Beach, gleaming white against the dark green of the bushy trees they were nestled amongst. Charmaine had caught the ferry over that morning. It was her day off, and she intended to take the money she'd earned by planning Penny and Rowan's wedding and buy herself a brand-new bike. The bicycle Betsy had given her was so old that the seat had finally rusted off and she could no longer justify riding around town without sitting down — it made her legs ache. Besides, she could easily hurt herself if someone stopped suddenly in front of her and she was forced back onto the rusty metal where the seat had previously been. So, with her newly made cash in hand, she strode down the side street to where the maps app had told her there was a bike shop.

It'd been a long time since she'd saved up to buy something on her own, and the satisfaction of doing that left her with a heady feeling. It wasn't as though she'd never been able to afford a large purchase before. She'd bought much more expensive things than a bike in her previous life. But these days, a bicycle was all she could afford.

The store was a large one, with gleaming bikes of every size and colour stacked up and down in aisles. Charmaine worried that if she bumped into one, the entire shop would go down like a line of dominoes. She stepped carefully between them, fingering handlebars, testing out seats and checking for kickstands.

"Can I help you with anything?" A pimply-faced teen boy asked the question.

She nodded. "I'm looking for a bike."

He grinned. "Well, you've come to the right place."

She laughed. "Yes, of course. Obviously."

"Any particular type of bike?"

"Well, I want one with gears so I can go up hills easily."

"That's a good start," the boy replied thoughtfully. "Anything else?"

"I'd like a basket to carry my cat in."

"Come this way," he said, leading her away from the mountain bikes she'd been perusing and over to a set of more upright bicycles with large baskets on the front.

In the end, she chose a bright red bicycle that gleamed beneath the florescent lighting. The salesman let her take it for a spin in the parking lot and she loved the feel of it. She couldn't believe how beautiful it was and that she'd get to ride it around the island. She also purchased some bike shorts and a Lycra top, helmet and tyre repair kit.

"I hope you enjoy your new ride," he said as he rang up her order.

She thanked him and wheeled her bike out onto the pavement, then slipped on her helmet and put the rest of her things in the basket. Then, with a quick jangle of the bell on her handlebars, she wove it through the pedestrians swarming down the street and rode back to the ferry terminal. It rolled smoothly and easily, the gears shifted quietly, and once she got the hang of it, she found climbing the small hills on her way back much more manageable.

By the time the ferry arrived on Coral Island, she'd familiarised herself with how to pump up the tyres, which gears were for what purpose, and how every part of that bike felt beneath her fingertips. She wheeled it off the ferry with a smile and then climbed aboard again to ride it back to her flat. When she arrived, she found Watson standing at the bottom of the stairs, tail curled around the pole. He'd recovered completely from the chocolate incident and seemed pleased to see her, miaowing loudly and pushing himself up against her legs as he purred.

She picked him up and hugged him, then placed him in the basket to see how he'd react. He sat, curled his tail around himself and acted as though it was the most natural place in the world for him to be — perched up high, ready to go on an adventure together.

At first, she rode slowly, looking to see how Watson would react. But he didn't move, instead staring ahead like a sentinel on guard. She laughed into the wind, standing on her pedals to push hard up a small rise, then onto the open road. She pedalled all the way to St James, the small township where Penny's animal refuge was located. The refuge looked to be closed, so she circled it once, then headed for home. On the way, she spotted Samantha, Betsy's granddaughter, playing on the side of the road. She pulled her bike to a stop and balanced it in place with her legs.

"Hi, Sam," she said.

Samantha looked up with a squint, recognised her and ran over to meet her. "You brought Watson!"

"I got a new bike. Don't you think he fits in the basket perfectly?"

Sam laughed and petted the cat, then scratched beneath his chin. "He loves it."

Sam's eyes were red-rimmed, and her cheeks splotched with red patches. Charmaine tipped her head to one side. "Is everything okay, Sam? Are you upset about something?"

The girl pulled back, her smile fading into a scowl. She crossed her arms. "I'm fine."

"Are you sure? Because you don't have to be fine. You can tell me if you're not."

"I'm sick of Dad being angry, that's all. He's angry all the time these days."

"What's he angry about?" Charmaine asked.

Sam kicked at a stone, sending it flying across the road. It skipped a few times before landing in the long grass on the other side. They both watched it go.

"I don't know. I guess he's angry about my mum. But also about Grandma. Says she's a liar and a fraud. I don't know what *fraud* means, but it must be bad because he yells at her on the phone a lot."

A man appeared nearby at a fence and shouted Samantha's name. Charmaine recognised him as Betsy's son. He waved Sam over, so Charmaine called out hello and raised a hand, hoping to put him at ease. It would be unnerving to see your child speaking to someone who appeared to be a stranger on the side of the road. But he seemed to recognise her as well and waved back.

"I've got to go," Sam said reluctantly, looking over her shoulder at her father.

"I hope things get better soon," Charmaine said. What else could she say? There wasn't anything she could do to help. "If you need anything, you can reach me at the shop."

"Thanks," Sam replied. "See you later."

"Okay."

Charmaine watched the girl run back to her father and duck through a gate into their yard. Her heart ached for the child. If only there was something she could do to help. She knew only too well how hard it was to be part of a family where secrets and emotions dominated.

The only thing she couldn't reconcile was how the sweet old lady who was her employer, her landlord, who had gifted her a bike and chatted amicably every day about all kinds of things while they worked, was the same lady described by her own son. There was no indication, to Charmaine's way of thinking, that Betsy would lie or defraud anyone. Everything she did seemed to be for the benefit of her son, her grand-daughter, her brother and even her employee. She rarely did anything for herself. What on earth were Sam and her father talking about?

As she rode back to Kellyville and her flat, she studied the trees lining the road, the birds flitting between them, the back of Watson's head in the basket before her, and thought about her new life on Coral Island. She'd left so much drama behind that she'd hoped not to find any more where she settled.

It'd been her goal to put down roots somewhere no one knew who she was, around people who had nothing to hide and no conflict in their lives. Betsy had seemed a safe bet. An elderly woman who was so sweet she made chocolate seem bitter. And yet there were serious issues in her family that Charmaine couldn't overlook.

She pulled her bike to a stop at the bottom of the steps that led up to her flat, then carried it gingerly upstairs, with Watson stalking along behind her. Inside the flat, she found a place to stash the bike where the old one had been before (she'd left it by the dumpster at the end of the street). Then she poured food into a bowl for Watson, made herself some macaroni and cheese and sat on the couch to read.

Watson curled up beside her once he'd finished his meal, and she patted him absently as she read. Finally, she put down the book and stared out the open window at the dark street beyond. There was more to this place than she'd believed at first. But whether she should stay long enough to discover what Coral Island was hiding, she hadn't yet decided.

Fourteen

BEATRICE PLACED a pot of tea and two cups with saucers on the small round table and slid into the seat across from Charmaine.

"Sorry I took so long. We've had a deluge of customers in the past hour."

Rain pounded against the café's roof so loud it was difficult to hear herself think, let alone Charmaine's voice as she murmured, "No worries. Let's talk about themes," Charmaine shuffled a pile of papers then handed one to Bea.

The paper had several different colour swatches and photographs of wedding styles and themes placed around the page. Bea glanced over each one, her pulse already accelerating. She'd been married before, done this already. She didn't want to have an over-the-top second wedding.

Aidan had suggested they get married in Italy, but she wasn't certain her friends and family would make the trip. Dad rarely flew to Sydney all the years when she lived there and Italy was a much longer flight than that. She wanted her loved ones at her wedding, it was really the only thing she cared about when it came to planning.

She pushed the paper aside. "I appreciate you going to the trouble. But the thing is, I don't really want a theme. I suppose the theme can be simple, classic, easy."

Charmaine nodded and chewed the end of a pencil. "I understand."

"I've been married before, and so has Aidan. We've been there, done that. We just want to make the commitment to each other to spend our lives together. We love each other, but we don't want a big fuss. It didn't help me the first time around, and it won't help now. All I care about is for Aidan and I vow to spend our lives together followed by a fun party. That's it."

Charmaine took notes, her face serious.

"I don't want to spend a tonne of money. We have better things to do with our cash, like travel or invest. And I don't like the idea of having a band. But I suppose we'll have to hire someone to play music for us."

"Maybe a DJ?" Charmaine suggested.

Bea grinned. "Yes, a DJ. I love the nineties classics and want to be able to dance without being deafened by a drum kit."

"I think we can find someone you'll be happy with."

Bea rubbed her hands down her skirt. "I really appreciate you doing this. I know you're busy. How is the cat?"

"Watson is as good as new."

"Glad to hear it."

Charmaine put her pencil down on the table and met Bea's gaze. "It seems like you're a bit nervous about the wedding."

"I am," Bea admitted. "I've been here before, and it didn't end well. I love Aidan, but what if it doesn't work out? I know you can't answer that. I'm sorry." She shook her head slowly.

Charmaine smiled. "Don't apologise—I understand. It's a big step to take. I think it must be normal to be anxious about it, at least a little bit. I've never been married myself, so I really can't say for sure. But since you're divorced, it makes sense you'd be hesitant to dive in again."

"The thing is — it feels fast, but it's not. We've known each other forever, and we were in love for a long time. If I'm being completely honest, I never lost that love for Aidan, and he's told me the same. So, the wedding has been a long time coming. Still, I'm starting to wonder if the proposal was rushed. We had a wonderful day together, and it was so romantic. He's so thoughtful and caring—it warmed my heart. I'm still not used to it, since Preston was never like that with me. And we got caught up in the moment."

"You don't think he planned the proposal?" Charmaine asked.

"I suppose he must've planned it, since he had the ring in his pocket." Bea's eyes narrowed as she thought it through. It might've been a surprise to her, but clearly it hadn't been unexpected for Aidan.

"It doesn't sound as though he was caught up in the moment, then," Charmaine said. "But if you have doubts..."

Bea drummed her fingertips on the table. Did she? Were the thoughts and feelings racing around inside her in that moment doubts or simply anxiety over the unknown future that lay before her? It would be so much easier to go through the rest of her life taking no chances, making no changes and simply existing in her cottage and working at the café. But how much of a life would that be?

"I don't have doubts. Aidan is the man I want to spend my life with."

Charmaine grinned. "I'm glad to hear it. You're a little anxious about the wedding, and it's my job to help alleviate that as much as possible."

"What do you suggest?"

"Your instinct is to have a small, intimate and simple

wedding. I think we should go with that. Let's not try to make it into something more."

Bea sighed with relief. "Yes, that's exactly what I need."

"I suggest you invite the minimum number of people, perhaps hold the ceremony outdoors — maybe on the beach. And have the reception at a restaurant where everything's already in place and you don't have to put in a lot of work to bring it all together."

"I like the sound of that. Thanks, Chaz."

Charmaine packed up her things and waved goodbye. Bea got back to work, already feeling the weight of her anxiety lifting. Marrying Aidan should be the best day of her life — she'd waited for this moment for decades. The last thing they both needed was to put too much pressure on themselves in order to have a perfect ceremony.

The first thing she should do was call Dani to ask her to be the maid of honour. She'd already decided not to have any other bridesmaids besides Aidan's daughter. Instead, her friends would be her only guests outside of her family. Aidan, too, planned only to invite his family and closest friends. He'd said he would ask Harry to be his best man, which warmed Bea's heart. She knew Harry would be thrilled. And she loved the idea of having both of her children involved in the ceremony.

She tugged her mobile phone from her skirt pocket and dialled Dani's number. Her daughter answered quickly.

"Hi, Mum."

"Hello, sweetie. I hope you're having a good day."

"Not too bad. Have you ever made an Indian dal?" Something crackled in the background.

"Um... No, I don't think so."

"It's harder than it looks."

"I didn't know you were into curries."

"Damien loves curry. He's learning how to cook samosas

and really wanted a dal, but he's busy grading papers, so I said I would make it for him. I'm making a red lentil one, but I'm not sure it's the right consistency."

Bea didn't even want to address the fact that her daughter was waiting hand and foot on a man so much older than herself. She knew she was being irrationally touchy about Dani's dating life, but there was something about the situation that irked her.

"Maybe you should let Damien figure out how to cook dal on his own."

Dani didn't reply right away, so Beatrice charged ahead, filling the silence with words. "I called to talk to you about something, actually."

"What is it, Mum, because I'm about to burn this thing, so I don't have long."

"As you know, Aidan proposed."

"I'm really happy for both of you," Dani said, sounding partially distracted.

"Will you be my maid of honour."

"Wow. Really?" Dani's voice became animated, and she laughed. "I would love that, Mum."

"We can pick out a dress together if you like, or you can buy one in Sydney before you come. I'm going to ask Aidan's daughter, Grace, to be a bridesmaid as well, so the two of you will need something to wear, although it doesn't have to match. We're keeping things very casual."

"How casual?" Dani asked. "Because I bought this sari the other day..."

"I'm not sure you could call a sari casual, honey," Bea interrupted in a chirpy voice. "Let's try a simple cocktail-style dress instead. We're going to be on the beach for the ceremony, though, so nothing too floaty."

"Can I bring Damien?" Dani asked.

And there it was. The question Bea had been dreading.

The last person in the world she wanted at her small, intimate and very personal wedding on the beach was the lecturer who had convinced her twenty-one-year-old daughter to give up her sensible nature in order to date him. Surely there was a rule against that at the university. What if they broke up and he decided to fail Dani? There was a conflict of interest her daughter didn't seem to see.

"I suppose there's no reason why not..." Bea said, not wanting a fight.

"It'll be good for you to meet him before we move in together. Did I tell you we're thinking of getting a flat?"

Bea leaned both elbows on the café counter. "A flat?"

"He's found this amazing two-bedroom flat we can rent. It's right next to the university and has this gorgeous swimming pool and a gym downstairs. It would be perfect for us, but I can't afford my share of the rent with my part-time café job so I might take a break from study to work full-time. I'm planning on switching to architecture anyway, and I'll need some money saved to really focus on my studies when I do that."

"What?" Anger flooded Bea's body, and her head spun. "He wants you to withdraw from your degree so you can work full time at a café and pay his rent?"

Dani groaned. "Mum, you've become such a fuddy-duddy lately. We're in love, and we *both* want to be together. Surely you of all people understand that."

Bea thought her head might explode. She didn't even know where to start. There were so many issues with what her daughter had said that it gave her a pounding headache.

"Aidan and I are both mature adults who've been through a lot — we know who we are and what we want out of life. He's not asking me to give up on my dreams to be with him. And you shouldn't consider doing that for a man who could very well be out of your life by next week. I raised you better than that."

Dani huffed. "Mum, where did your sense of romance go?"

"I think it ran away with your father's mistress," Bea replied, then clamped a hand over her mouth. What was she doing? Preston's actions had nothing to do with their daughter. She shouldn't be taking out her frustrations, pain and mistrust on Dani.

"That's not fair, Mum," Dani said. "I'm going to go before I burn this curry."

She hung up the phone before Beatrice could protest. Bea closed her eyes and inhaled a slow breath through her nostrils. What was she thinking, talking to Dani that way? She'd been young and impulsive once. Since then, she'd endured a lot, and it had hardened her heart, given her a cynicism she'd never thought possible.

She wanted to protect Dani from heartbreak, but she didn't want to shield her from life entirely. Life was often found in the absence of planning or common sense — instead, joy came from the unexpected, the connections and the love stories no one saw coming. What if she stepped in and prevented Dani from finding her own great love, like the one she shared with Aidan?

Just then, one of the waitresses dropped an entire tray of glasses, still hot from the dishwasher. The tray fell to the floor with a gigantic crash of breaking glass. Everyone in the café looked up in surprise. Bea's heart almost leapt from her chest. She hurried to survey the damage, her heart thundering against her rib cage, and found that every single glass on the tray had been broken.

She pressed both hands to her hips and used every ounce of self restraint to keep from cursing out loud.

The waitress, a teenager who'd recently begun doing afternoon shifts at the café, regarded her with wide eyes, lower lip trembling.

"I'm sorry, Mrs Rushton," she said.

Bea pushed a smile onto her face. "It was an accident. You can wait tables, and I'll clean this up."

Sometimes she wished she could turn back time and keep her pigtailed little girl at home. The two of them could bake cupcakes and decorate them with sprinkles, watch Play School and take a nap. Times were simpler then. Now, she had no control over the way Dani lived her life and had to trust the decisions she made. Something that was much easier said than done.

Fifteen

BEA'S COFFEE was closed but the atmosphere was festive. Charmaine set everything they needed out in neat piles on the tables that'd been pushed together in the centre of the café. There were stacks of menus, piles of ribbon already cut into uniform lengths, place settings with calligraphy in a stunning matte black ink with the guest's name, mounds of cut flowers and more. It was an assembly line to prepare for Penny and Rowan's wedding that weekend, and the entire bridal party was pitching in.

"Champagne all around!" Beatrice cried as she carried a bottle to the table and handed around champagne flutes. "We're celebrating."

"There's nothing more fun than a group craft project," Evie said, clapping her hands together.

Taya's eyes widened. "You're always so chipper, Evie. I don't know how you do it."

Evie pouted. "I'm not being chipper—I really do love crafting. Add in friends, and what more could I want?"

Taya laughed.

Penny pushed a handful of glue sticks onto the table. "And I for one am grateful you feel that way, sweetie. It's one of the reasons why we all love you."

"That and your never-ending supply of good books," Bea added with a wink as she poured champagne.

"And here I was thinking it was my sparkling brown eyes," Evie said with a flutter of black lashes.

"You know, this is the first time we've all been able to get together in weeks," Penny said, slumping into a chair with a sigh. "It's so good to see you. I'm exhausted, but I've been looking forward to tonight anyway."

Each took a glass of champagne and raised it in a toast, then drank.

"Hear, hear," said Bea.

"Taya's job is taking her away from us far too much," Penny continued. "But I couldn't be happier for you, honey. So, let's toast to friendship."

"To friendship," they shouted as they touched glasses together and then drank again.

"And to Penny and Rowan. May they have everlasting love and happiness," Bea replied.

They all said "cheers" again and toasted their friends.

One of the waitresses from the café strode from the kitchen with two trays of food and set them on the table, then waved her goodbyes before closing the door behind her. She stepped out into the darkening evening just as Betsy climbed the stairs, almost entirely hidden by an armful of cut native flowers. She pushed through the door with her rear end, then spun about and teetered across the floor to where the ladies sat.

Charmaine leapt to her feet to help Betsy with one hand on her arm. "You shouldn't be doing this yourself. Why didn't you give me a call?"

Betsy set the flowers down in the only empty space she could find and waved a hand in protest. "Never mind all that. I'm not an invalid yet."

"Yes, I know, but you could've tripped."

"Well, I didn't." Betsy's eyes sparkled, and she smiled at Charmaine. "All's well that ends well. Here are the rest of the flowers for the table settings. I wish you ladies luck this evening pulling it all together. I'm sure you won't need it, since it looks to me like you're doing a fantastic job. I miss those days of girlfriends getting married and sitting together until the wee hours doing the last-minute chores and errands. But I hope you all have the best of times and get plenty of sleep." She winked.

They thanked her. Charmaine offered her a glass of champagne, which she turned down.

"When you get to my age, you have to think twice about everything you eat or drink, especially before bedtime. Which, for me, is in a few minutes, so I'll bid you all adieu."

Beatrice cleared her throat. "Betsy, I hope you don't mind. But I've been meaning to ask you a question."

Betsy had already turned to walk away. She spun back slowly, her eyes filled with curiosity. "I don't mind at all, honey. Shoot."

"It's nothing, really." She exchanged a look with her friends. Penny seemed uncomfortable. Evie appeared confused, but Taya urged her on with a nod of her head.

Charmaine had no idea what Beatrice was referring to, but she watched with curiosity as Beatrice reached for a thank-you card and began awkwardly attempting to thread a piece of cream-coloured ribbon through a small circular hole in the top of the card.

"As you know, I found a box of items a few months ago in a cave down by the ocean near my cottage. I've asked the police to give me some insight into what I found, but they simply tell me it's an ongoing investigation and they can't comment on it."

"Oh, yes. I'd forgotten about that," Betsy replied, her smile faltering.

"There was a driver's licence in the box, with your brother Buck's photo on it. But the thing I'm confused about is the name on the licence — it wasn't Buck. It was Samuel Jay Gilmore. The address was in California."

Betsy didn't reply, simply bobbed her head.

Bea continued, her voice softer. "I suppose I was wondering what his real name is and why it would be different now to what was written on that old licence."

Betsy pressed her hands together. Her purple silk kaftan glimmered in the soft lighting, and her eyes appeared to reflect the same colour back to them. "His name was Samuel—it's true. I'm not sure how his licence ended up in an odd box of items hidden in a cave. It's almost like a children's mystery book, isn't it?" She laughed, but the sound was hollow.

"Why did he change it?" Taya asked.

Betsy shrugged. "We both changed our names when we moved to Australia. It was a long time ago, and we've left that part of our lives behind us. But if you must know, we were raised in a cult. It wasn't a happy time for either of us, and we've done our best to put it behind us."

"Which cult was it?" Bea asked.

Betsy's cheeks pinked. "I'm sure you can understand that I'd prefer not to go into details. It was so long ago, I honestly feel like a completely different person to the one who moved away looking for a new beginning. Buck has changed as well — he isn't that person anymore. We escaped from a life we didn't want any longer, and we've built something for ourselves here. The police know all about it. They've spoken with us both extensively."

Beatrice smiled. "That makes a lot of sense. Thanks for telling us, Betsy. I'm glad the two of you managed to find your way out of that."

"Thank you, honey. It's been a trek, for sure. Anyway, you ladies have a lovely night."

Betsy told them all goodbye then left them alone in the café. The women were quiet as they got to work organising place settings and composing flower arrangements for the tables.

"What do you think about all that?" Penny asked suddenly.

Bea shrugged. "I think it makes sense. I can understand why they'd want to change their names and start again somewhere new if they were escaping a toxic environment."

"A cult? It's so bizarre," Taya said. "I don't know..."

"I can imagine Betsy in a cult," Evie added as she reached for a place setting. "She's so nice, I think she'd be easily convinced. Plus, she's into wearing kaftans and eating organic — maybe it was one of those hippy commune kind of cults."

Charmaine had remained quiet throughout the entire conversation, processing everything she'd heard and seen. Betsy's words rang true to her. It certainly explained some of the things that'd confused her about her boss, the situation with Betsy's son and granddaughter, and the friction between them.

But why had it taken so long for Betsy to share the truth with her friends and neighbours? Perhaps she'd carried the shame of what they'd been a part of all these years. Charmaine couldn't figure out if Betsy was protecting a guilty brother or fighting for an innocent one. But whatever the motivation, she was clearly a sister who wanted to protect her brother.

"We should talk about a wet weather plan," she said, changing the subject abruptly.

Penny's lips pursed. "No, it's not going to rain. I forbid it."

Charmaine laughed. "I hope it doesn't, of course, but there is a storm forecast, so we should think about what we'll do if it's raining during the ceremony, since you're getting married on the headland at Point Prospect. If there's too much rain or wind, we won't be able to manage it, I'm afraid. The reception is at the Blue Shoal Inn, so that's covered. But we need to think about the ceremony."

Penny shook her head. "Nope, it's going to be fine. There's no Plan B. Plan A is all we have. I'm pretty good at predicting the weather, and I can feel it in my bones — it's going to be sunny and warm. Besides, we want the island to be part of our ceremony. It will mean so much to both of us to be standing on the beach when we say our vows."

Bea and Taya exchanged a concerned look.

Bea arched an eyebrow. "That's really romantic. And we all hope for fine weather, sweetie. But you need a wet weather plan. Everyone has a wet weather plan when they get married outdoors. It's perfectly normal."

Just then, Rowan stepped into the café and shut the door quietly behind him. He carried three pizza boxes over to the tables and set them down near Penny before leaning over to kiss her.

"I can't think about that right now," Penny said.

"Think about what?" Rowan asked.

"We're talking about a wet weather plan for the wedding," Charmaine replied.

"That's a good idea. I hear there might be a storm," Rowan said.

Penny shot him a look of frustration.

"What?" he asked with a laugh. "Did I say something wrong?"

"I don't believe it'll rain. I'm holding out for sunshine."

He sighed. "Okay, honey. That's fine — don't you worry about it. I'll take care of it."

"Thank you," Penny said, immediately perking up. "But the weather is going to be perfect."

Sixteen

THE WIND that whipped around the point and along the beach outside her house in the early hours of the morning made Penny's heart thump a little faster than usual. She walked onto the deck, wrapped in her bathrobe, and stared over the ocean as she sipped her morning coffee.

She was getting married today.

Nerves fluttered in the pit of her stomach as a wave of excitement rolled through her body. They would finally be husband and wife after so many years of back and forth. She was ashamed it'd taken her so long to see what was right in front of her — that Rowan Clements was the man she loved.

She'd always felt that way about him, she realised now. But she'd pushed him away with their little spats and disagreements. He irritated her because he got under her skin in a way she didn't know how to process. But now that she'd finally accepted her own feelings, she'd never been happier. And everything would be perfect as long as the weather didn't change.

At that moment, dark clouds skidded across the sky, blocking out the rising sun. The wind changed direction and buffeted the coastline. She shivered and pulled her robe more tightly around her body.

Taya slipped through the back door of the beach house and looped an arm around Penny's shoulders. "The weather isn't looking great."

"No, but it'll be fine. We only need half an hour for the ceremony. Surely it won't rain until this afternoon."

"Surely not," Taya said.

"I'm getting married."

"Yes, you are. And the two of you are going to be blissfully happy together."

"You think so? I'm not the easiest person in the world to live with. And I've never lived with a man, other than my step-dad, before now."

"You'll be fine. You've lived with your brother, Rob."

"That's true, but only for short stints, and he drives me crazy."

Taya laughed. "I have no experience with siblings, but I've heard that's normal. You and Rowan love each other, and you're going to be okay. You'll fight, everyone does, but when you love each other, you can work it out."

"He's giving up so much. What if he stops believing I'm worth it?"

"There is no true love without sacrifice. It costs each one of us to love someone well. Whether it's giving up nights out on the town, or resisting the urge to spend all your money on sheep collectibles, or sacrificing time we could be recharging in order to listen to someone's hard day, or rising from bed early in the morning to drive a child to Little Athletics training..."

"I remember you doing that for Camden," Penny interjected.

"That's right, and even though I hated getting up before the sun while it was cold outside, I did it because I loved her. Love and sacrifice are never far apart. He's giving something up for you now, but you'll do the same for him. That's how marriage works. Now, let's eat some breakfast with Bea and Evie before they devour all the pancakes. We've got a busy day ahead."

* * *

Seated in the car at Point Prospect, Penny stared out the window of the minivan. Rain lashed the vehicle as the wind howled around the headland. Palm trees waved their fronds and dove towards the earth with every gust of wind. She wore a pair of jeans and a T-shirt, with her makeup and hair already done. She'd planned to change into her dress on site so she didn't wrinkle the fabric. A small white veil hung over the back of her hair, which was pulled into a loose chignon with curls draped down either side of her face.

"It's not looking good, honey," Taya said, seated behind her. "What do you want to do?"

Penny choked back a sob. "The wedding's in an hour. Do you think it will clear up?" She knew the answer. She'd lived on the island her entire life. This storm had set in and wasn't going anywhere. Still, she hoped Taya might give a different answer and assuage her anxiety.

"It's here to stay, I'm afraid."

Bea leaned forwards from the back seat. "Did you ever come up with a wet weather plan?"

"Rowan said he'd take care of it, remember," Charmaine added. She was in the driver's seat, her lap covered in a box of bouquets she was checking to make sure they hadn't been squashed on the drive over. She leaned back to put the bouquets on the floor in front of Taya.

Penny nodded mutely.

"I'm going to give him a call, okay?" Charmaine spoke in the voice people generally reserved for emotional children or crazy people. Penny had heard it a hundred times before when Taya used it on guests at the inn, or the voice Penny had adopted to de-escalate frightened visitors to the refuge when an animal did something unexpected. But it didn't matter — she needed the calming resonance to help her manage the frantic thoughts jumbled about in her head.

It was her wedding day, and the tropical island had decided to throw a massive hissy fit with a tropical storm like they'd not seen in months. Most days on the island were sunny and clear. But as the time of the wedding approached, the sky had only became darker and more foreboding. Now, they could barely hear one another over the thunder of rain on the mini-van's roof.

"At least you're having the reception at the Inn," Bea said, in a comforting voice.

"It'll withstand any storm," Taya added. "We finished the renovation just in time, so everything looks fresh and new."

"It's stunning," Bea said with a nod.

"Thank you, honey," Taya replied.

Charmaine held the phone to her ear and shouted back and forth with Rowan for several minutes, repeating herself regularly and blocking her other ear with a fingertip. Penny didn't try to keep up with what she was saying, instead focusing her attention on the sodden white chairs resting in a line against the timber fencing around the headland. The equipment hire company had set the chairs out on the grass, then retreated to the shelter of the truck when the rain squall hit.

"I should never have planned an outdoor wedding," Penny said.

Bea patted her arm. "I'm definitely rethinking the choice for my own wedding."

Charmaine hung up the phone. "Okay, change of plans. We're going to Aidan's house."

"What?" Bea asked, sitting up straight.

Charmaine grinned. "Your fiancé has agreed to let us hold the wedding at his brand-new house down the street."

Bea sighed. "That's perfect. It's close by, there's plenty of space, and plus, he has that enormous enclosed back deck."

Penny felt like she might cry. It was so kind of Aidan to allow them to use his space last minute, but how would they manage to get everything set up, all the decorations in place, and let the guests know about the change of plans in less than one hour?

Charmaine squeezed her hand. "Aidan said to tell you not to worry about a thing. It's all taken care of. We can pull into the garage so you won't get wet. Henry is already there helping to set up, so all we have to do is drive over."

Penny had a thousand questions she wanted to ask, but she felt so deflated, she couldn't bring herself to do it. None of it would work out — the guests would be lost, the ceremony nothing like what she'd pictured. But at least she had Rowan, her parents and her friends. The rest of it didn't matter in the end.

Charmaine started the van, and they drove the short distance to Aidan's house. Meanwhile, Penny stared out the window and did her best to calm her nerves with deep breathing. In the seats behind her, Bea and Evie discussed with Charmaine the best places to get photographs at Aidan's house. Beatrice called her father, who was doing the photography for Penny and Rowan free of charge as his gift to them since Evie was in the wedding party, and told him to meet them at Aidan's.

"This isn't a sign, is it?" Penny asked, her anxiety returning.

Charmaine pulled the van into Aidan's driveway. The garage door lifted automatically.

Taya spoke up. "No, it's not a sign of anything but weather. Weather happens."

"You're sure?"

"I'm certain."

Charmaine parked the minivan in the garage, and Aidan opened the sliding door to help Bea, Taya and Evie step out. Penny was about to open her own door when it was pulled open and she found herself staring up into Rowan's green eyes. They crinkled around the edges as he smiled and held out a hand for her to take.

She placed her hand in his and stepped out of the minivan, a lump forming in her throat.

"You look beautiful," he said.

"We're not supposed to see each other," she objected even as a rush of relief washed over her at the sight of him.

He wrapped his arms around her and held her close while gazing into her eyes. "I knew you might be feeling a little upset about the weather, so I wanted to give you a hug and tell you it's all going to be okay. Better than okay — it's going to be great. I've sorted it all out. The guests will be arriving here on time, the entire place is decorated, the minister is already seated in the living room eating snacks and telling dad jokes. And I can't wait to marry you."

"How did you do it all so quickly?"

"We've been working on it for hours, but I couldn't reach you to let you know."

"I can't find my phone," she said, with a sigh.

He laughed. "Well, you have a dozen messages on it."

His hair was combed perfectly, chestnut waves with streaks of grey that made him look distinguished. He wore a pair of jeans and a soft blue T-shirt. There were drips of rainwater on his shoulders. He smelled like cologne and minty gum.

"Thank you," she whispered, standing on tiptoe to kiss him.

"Go upstairs. There's a room all set up for you ladies to get dressed in. There's a bottle of champagne and some fruit and other snacks for you. If you need anything else, just yell. Aidan's locked Nelly in the laundry room, so if you hear scratching, ignore it. She's fine and surrounded with chew toys and snacks."

* * *

By the time the ceremony began, Penny's anxiety had abated and all she felt was pure joy. Rowan and his groomsmen had brought all the decorations to the house. They'd contacted the equipment rental company, who'd come and set up the chairs in Aidan's living room. The flowers were placed along a makeshift aisle. The minister stood before floor-to-ceiling picture windows that held a silent vigil over the ocean even as the rain subsided.

Penny walked down the staircase behind her bridesmaids with one hand resting on her stepfather's arm. Henry patted her hand, then steadied himself with the handrail as they made their descent. The small group of guests turned to watch her as a string quartet played Pachelbel's Canon.

Rowan wore a black suit without a tie, his white shirt unbuttoned at the collar. His green eyes glistened as he watched her descend the staircase, his lips pulled into a wide smile. She breathed deeply, savouring the moment. There had been a time in her twenties when she was desperate to find someone, to settle down and get married. She'd dated a man for five years, hoping he'd pop the question someday, but looking back, she knew they weren't a good match. And he must've known it as well because he never asked and then ended their relationship. She'd been devastated at the time, wondering how she could've wasted so much time on someone who clearly didn't love her the way she longed to be loved.

But now, she saw the truth. He wasn't the one for her. All these years, Rowan had been there in the back of her mind, returning to the island during his holidays, teasing her, irritating her, visiting Rob and making excuses to stay longer to spend time with her. She hadn't recognised her true feelings for such a long time, but now she'd finally given in to them, and she felt more joy and peace over their future together than she ever had.

She paced slowly down the shallow aisle. Henry, kissed her cheek and Rowan took her hand. Rowan's eyes were shimmering with tears, but her own were clear. She didn't feel like crying now. She felt like laughing instead. Laughing with joy.

"Do you take this man?" the minister asked.

She let out a burst of giggles, then shouted, "Yes!"

Everyone in the audience laughed along with her. Then when she threw her arms around Rowan's neck to kiss him after they were pronounced husband and wife, the entire group cheered.

Seventeen

TWO DAYS LATER, Charmaine rode her new bike around the island after a full day of work in the florist shop. She'd been so busy with weddings every weekend, she hadn't had the chance to do much exploring. Since she'd worked on Saturday for Penny's wedding, delivering the flowers and planning the event, Betsy had let her finish work early today. She'd collected Watson, sat him in the basket on the front of her bike and set off to pedal as far as she could manage.

The sun was shining. All the world was glistening after the rain. Grass blades bent double beneath droplets of water, the roads were pockmarked with muddy puddles, and birds swooped and sang, glad to be flying free once again.

She felt much the same way. It was good to be outside, on her own and able to go wherever she wished. She enjoyed her work, but needed a break. And what better way to spend her free time than on her shiny new bike with Watson in the basket?

The cat had sheltered out the storm in the seat of her armchair, curled into a ball with eyes firmly shut. He'd blinked sleepily in her direction when she'd come inside after the wedding, shaking the droplets of water from her umbrella. Then with a yawn, he went back to sleep. She didn't mind. It was nice to have someone to come home to.

The road dipped before climbing a low hill. Then she stopped at the small cove where she'd met up with Beatrice and Aidan swimming. She carried Watson down to the water's edge and walked through the lapping waves, letting the water splash as high as her thighs. Watson wasn't keen on that, so she retreated back up the beach before he covered her arms with scratches. He soon settled down, and she watched as a small flock of seagulls circled overhead and landed close by, hoping she might have something for them to eat.

The tension of the past few years had worn her down. It'd been so long since she'd felt this relaxed, and she wasn't exactly sure what to do with herself. It was as though for the first time in a long time, she could simply *be* rather than doing anything in particular. She wasn't looking over her shoulder, wasn't thinking about what she might've done differently, wasn't regretting her actions. If she let herself think too deeply, she'd go there again. Instead she watched the waves lapping against the golden sand, closed her eyes to enjoy the warmth of the sun on her face.

Her thoughts kept returning to the original reason she'd moved to Coral Island.

Her aunt.

Even if Charmaine could locate her, would she want to know her? The extended family had given up on her mother a long time ago. It was unlikely they'd want anything to do with Charmaine.

She carried Watson back to the bike. The cat was eager to get into the basket. She didn't want him leaping out in the middle of nowhere, so she hurried to get the bike going again, pedalling in the direction of Kellyville.

The truth was, there was a quiet hoping deep down inside

that perhaps on her daily jaunts she might see her aunt and recognise her immediately — she could look like her own mother, or have her voice, or her laugh. But in the weeks that she'd lived on the island, she hadn't encountered anyone who fit that description.

If her mother hadn't severed the connection, maybe Charmaine would've been raised in a large, extended family who spent their days fishing, snorkelling and sunbathing. Nothing like the city life she'd grown up with—the smog, traffic, hordes of people pushing their way onto the train to get to school or work. How different her life might've been.

Back on the main street of Kellyville, she pulled her bike to a stop in front of the florist shop. Betsy was still inside serving customers. There was no sign of Sam, who used to come after school every day, but who Charmaine hadn't seen all week. The sun beat on her shoulders. Sweat dripped a trail down the middle of her spine. Watson immediately leapt from the basket as soon as the bike rolled to a halt and disappeared down the alley beside the shop.

"We're going to have to talk about your attitude, mister," she called after him. Absolutely no gratitude, she thought with a giggle.

She pushed the bike towards the alley, but one last glance down the street and she froze in place. There was a group of tourists milling about the doorway to Bea's Coffee. The back of a brown haired man had caught her attention and sent a chill along her spine. She stared at his head even as it spun in her direction.

"Chaz!" A feminine voice called her name from the other direction.

She blanched and shrank back into the alley so she was hidden by the brick wall of the florist shop.

Directly opposite her, Evie raised a hand over her head, and Bea shot her a quizzical look. She waved discreetly at them both, then peeked out from behind the wall. The man she'd seen was staring in her direction. He'd heard her name called and scanned the street with purpose, then stepped through the crowd to see better.

She pushed the bike to the back of the building where the entrance to her flat was located. Footsteps pounded across the street. She turned the corner at the back of the shop and waited. Bea and Evie weren't far behind.

Bea's eyebrows drew low, her forehead creased. "Chaz, are you okay? You've turned very pale."

"You look sick, sweetie. Maybe you should sit down." Evie's face was lined with concern.

"I'm fine, really." She had to get rid of them, and that meant feigning good health. In that moment, she was light-headed and had a pang of irritation and anxiety in her chest that grew more painful by the moment.

She was accustomed to panic attacks; she'd had them often enough over the past few years. What she needed was to get inside the flat, sit down and do some breathing exercises or a mediation. Instead, all she could think about was that man in the street and whether he'd followed the two women standing in front of her now.

"Let's go upstairs," she suggested, scanning the alleyway behind them.

Bea and Evie helped Charmaine carry her bike up the stairs. She unlocked the back door and went inside. Then she sat in the armchair, staring at the wall and working on her breathing.

Evie shut the door behind them.

"I get panic attacks sometimes. That's all," Charmaine said after a while.

Bea had already put the kettle on to boil, and Evie was searching the fridge for something for Charmaine to eat.

"I found half a camembert and some crackers," she said, holding the fridge door open. "Will that do?"

"That would be great," Charmaine said, although she really wasn't hungry.

Before long, she was presented with a coffee by Bea and a plate of cheese and crackers by Evie. Then both women perched on the edge of the couch and watched as she took a sip.

"Who was that man?" Bea asked suddenly.

Charmaine's heart skipped a beat. "What man?"

"The one you were looking at when all the blood left your face."

She took another sip of coffee. "Oh, him? That's my brother, Sean."

Evie and Bea looked at each other in confusion.

"I thought your brother was missing."

"He was... I guess he's not any longer." Charmaine took a bite of cracker, letting the flavour of the camembert linger in her mouth before swallowing.

"Why weren't you happy to see him? He's been missing, I thought you were concerned about him."

"I was concerned. But I don't really want to see him. It's complicated." The fact was, she didn't know how to go about telling her new friends the truth. Nor did she want to. They'd caught her off guard, and she was lightheaded over having seen Sean outside her flat. Complicated didn't begin to describe their situation, her family dynamics and the way she felt about her brother. It was so typical of him to show up like this and expect she'd want to see him.

"I don't understand," Bea replied, her voice warm with compassion. "But you don't have to tell us anything you don't want to. You should know that we're here for you. Okay?"

Relief swamped Charmaine. Their friendship meant more to her than they could ever understand. "Thank you."

"We can stay if you'd like," Evie offered.

"No, I'm fine. I think I'll lie down for a few minutes and get some rest."

"Okay. Call if we can help."

Both women left, and Charmaine locked the door and the cat door behind them. Watson was in for the night, already crouched in the kitchen eating his dinner from the bowl on the floor. She ran her hand along his back, and he arched beneath it, purring at her touch.

Perhaps it was time to move on again, although she'd finally found somewhere she felt at home. How had Sean located her? And why had he come? Anger darkened her thoughts. She should've changed her name, but she didn't think he was looking for her. Clearly, he was fine and yet had still abandoned her. He didn't deserve to see her.

The way he'd left things between them — she had suspicions about his behaviour. Nothing concrete, nothing she could prove or put her finger on, simply a feeling, a squirmy discontent in the pit of her gut whenever she thought about him.

He'd disappeared, and she'd assumed she wouldn't hear from him again. Now that he was on the island, all she could think about was fleeing. But what would that achieve? He might simply follow her. He must be there for a reason — what did he want?

Her phone jangled, and she answered without thinking. When Sean said hello, her breath caught in her throat. She hung up the phone with a rush of adrenaline, then threw it onto the couch and stared at it in surprise. How had he found her number? He must know where she lived. There was no other explanation. She wasn't ready to talk to him yet, needed time to gather her thoughts, to consider what she'd say.

She ran to the window and pulled the curtains shut, then hurried to push a dining chair beneath the door handle.

Perhaps she was being overly dramatic. After all, he was her brother. But there was so much she didn't understand. So many things about him she didn't know. There were times it felt as if he was a stranger.

When her phone rang again, she turned it off, then went to bed with the lights on.

Eighteen

THE CAFÉ WAS empty when Charmaine walked through the front door the following evening. Beatrice was sweeping the floor. The chairs were upside down on all of the tables but one. Evie sat on that chair, sipping a cup of tea and looking over some paperwork. The last of the waitresses brushed past her with a wave and whooshed out the door as Charmaine made her way across the floor to sit with Evie. Outside, the afternoon sun sat low over the ocean, giving the entire town an orange glow.

"Have you heard from Penny and Rowan?" Evie asked.

Charmaine shook her head. "No, they're on their honeymoon in New Zealand, so I don't expect to hear anything. I'm sure they're having a great time."

"I haven't called or texted," Bea said, joining them at the table with a large casserole dish in her hands. "I don't want to disturb them." She set the dish down on the table with a grunt. "I brought you a lasagne."

Charmaine looked at Evie, then held a hand to her chest. "Who? Me?"

Bea laughed. "Yes, you. You're new to the island, so I

thought I'd make you a lasagne. I'm sorry I took so long. My allergies have been giving me so much trouble lately, but I'm finally feeling a lot better."

"That's so nice. Thank you." Charmaine looked at the lasagne through a veil of tears. No one had ever brought her a meal before.

"You're welcome. Since we're here to talk about weddings and food, it made me hungry thinking about it. And when I'm hungry, I cook."

"I can't believe you made something in your downtime when you have to do so much food prep here in the café," Evie said with a shake of her head.

"Well, I enjoy it. Besides, I wanted to do something nice for Chaz. Are you feeling any better after what happened yesterday?"

"Yes, thank you. I feel fine today."

"Did you ever speak to your brother?" Evie asked.

"Sean called my phone," Charmaine said. "I have no idea how he got the number."

Bea cleared her throat, then pointed at the bulletin board on the wall of the café. Charmaine slapped a palm to her forehead. "Of course, my flyer. I left my number on the notice board, advertising myself as a wedding planner. He must've seen it."

"Did you speak to him?" Evie asked.

Charmaine shook her head. "I hung up the phone."

"Maybe you should find out what he wants," Bea suggested. "Unless you're afraid of him for some reason."

"No, I'm not afraid." Charmaine was angry more than anything. Maybe all he wanted was to reconnect as a family. "I don't know if I want to talk to him, but I suppose I'll have to eventually. He's my brother — he came all this way for a reason. I guess I should find out what it is."

They spent the next hour talking through Bea's upcoming

wedding. Charmaine took notes and made suggestions. Beatrice and Aidan were two of the nicest people she'd ever met, and she was excited to be able to help them tie the knot.

At first, they'd intended on a simple beach wedding. But after the fiasco of Penny and Rowan's wedding, Bea had decided she didn't need the stress an outdoor ceremony. Charmaine understood how she felt — Penny's wedding had come close to giving her a stomach ulcer, and she wasn't even the bride.

So, Bea had changed the venue to the Blue Shoal Inn. They could get married in the rose garden outside the inn, or in the gazebo. Both settings were equally romantic, but Charmaine really loved the rose garden and hoped she selected that.

If the weather was bad, Taya promised they could easily move it inside. The guest list would be small enough for the inn to accommodate, and it was Charmaine's job to call the resort and confirm the request. She'd already made a tentative booking, and since there was only one weekend available, she'd snapped it up quickly, hoping Bea wouldn't change her mind.

Before she left, Evie pressed an old book into her hands. "I noticed you always carry a book with you. Try this one — it's one of my favourites."

"Thanks," Charmaine said. "I'll bring it back when I'm finished."

"We read it for book club last month. Everyone loved it. You should think about joining. We meet every month in the bookshop. It's a lot of fun."

"That sounds really nice," Charmaine replied, dropping the book into her shoulder bag. She waved goodbye to the women and stepped outside into the darkening twilight.

A book club was just the type of thing she never would've joined in her previous life. She wasn't a joiner, and did everything she could to avoid groups and clubs. It was her introversion but also insecurity that kept her at arm's length from the people around her.

These days, she didn't like being so distant. It was time she took a risk and put herself in situations that made connection possible, but also gave her some enjoyment in life. A book club might be just the thing she was looking for — she enjoyed reading, and it would open her up to meeting new people. She decided she would give it a try.

Rather than going directly home to her empty flat, Charmaine took a walk around the water's edge and along the dock, carrying the lasagna in both hands. The sun had set, and all that remained was a faint yellow glow above the mainland to show where it had been. The water was as black as ink as she stared across it. She shivered and looked up at the sky as the first stars began to shimmer faintly overhead.

"Not cold, are you?" A man's deep voice startled her from behind.

She spun around to find herself staring up into the large brown eyes of a very tall, athletic-looking man. He chuckled, and one side of his mouth pulled into a teasing grin.

"You gave her a fright, Bradford. I'm going to have to teach you some better manners when you're talking to people. Sorry about that, Chaz," Aidan said, coming up behind the other man and slapping him on the shoulder.

Aidan carried a small esky in one hand. The stranger held a long fishing rod.

Charmaine swallowed down her fright. She really shouldn't be so jumpy, but ever since her brother showed up, she expected him to jump out of a dark corner at any moment. "It's okay—I'm a little on edge. Not your fault. Have you been fishing?"

"We went spearfishing with Elias, Bea's dad." Aidan waved down the dock at an elderly man who was tying a boat in place.

"And mine..." Bradford added.

"Yes, yours too. But Chaz knows Beatrice."

"You know my sister?" Bradford asked.

"I'm planning her wedding."

"I'm Bradford," the man said, holding out a hand.

She shook his hand. "I'm Charmaine, but everyone calls me Chaz."

"You must be new in town."

"I've been living here a few weeks. Working at the florist shop with Betsy."

"Oh, right," Bradford said. "That must be why I haven't seen you around. I don't buy flowers often."

"What he means is, he's single," Aidan said with a wink as he strode back to the boat.

Charmaine smiled. "Did you catch anything?"

"We did okay. Now comes the not-so-fun part, cleaning the fish. But at least we'll have something good for dinner tonight."

"Sounds delicious. I love fresh fish."

"You should join us," Bradford offered.

"Oh, no, thanks. I wouldn't want to intrude. Besides, I have plans with Watson to eat this delicious lasagna made by your lovely sister."

"Your boyfriend?" Bradford asked, watching her intently.

She laughed. "No, my cat. I've got to get home to feed him or he might destroy my armchair. He likes to sharpen his claws on the fabric for some reason, especially if I'm late getting his dinner."

"Come on, Brad, you're not getting out of cleaning the fish this time," Elias shouted from the other end of the dock.

Bradford glanced back at his father impatiently. "Well, maybe you could come fishing with us next time."

"I'd love that," Charmaine replied.

She watched Bradford walk away. He looked over his

shoulder at her once before heading off in the direction of the fish cleaning station nearby. Aidan and Elias joined him, and the three of them got to work. Charmaine sat on the end of the dock for a few minutes watching the quiet water sloshing against the pylons until the last vestiges of the sunset were gone and the town was bathed in darkness.

There were a few streetlights still glowing when she walked back through the town to her flat above the florist's. Upstairs, she caught Watson with his claws embedded in the fabric at the base of the armchair, his back stretched out. He looked up at her when she opened the door without the slightest trace of guilt on his sleepy face.

"No, Watson," she said in frustration. "Step away from the armchair. That fabric isn't going to sharpen your claws." Perhaps she should make him some kind of claw sharpening station so he'd leave her furniture alone.

She fed him quickly and took his attention away from the chair. Then she heated up a large slice of lasagna for herself and placed the rest of it in the fridge. With only one person to feed, it was likely to last for days.

It reminded her of the casserole and lasagna dishes that'd piled up on the hall table before her mother's funeral. Mum's former colleagues, friends, and neighbours, as well as people who knew Charmaine, dropped by with their condolences and often with a dish of food.

Once they handed over the dish, they didn't seem to know what to do. They shuffled in place, unable to make eye contact for long. Whispered a few platitudes, then scurried back to their cars. There were a few people who remained longer, held conversations with her, showed genuine concern for her wellbeing.

It was amazing to Charmaine how quickly loss and grief revealed who was able to handle the pain of others and who couldn't face it. It thinned the crowd in a rapid fashion until she came to the realisation that there was nothing and no one worth remaining in Newcastle for after the funeral. No need to stay there any longer. Without her mother, it didn't feel like home.

The lasagna was delightful and melted in her mouth, cheese oozing from the béchamel sauce. The new book in her shoulder bag cried out for her attention, so she sat at the small dining table and opened it up to read. When she was mid paragraph, her mobile phone rang. She set down the book and answered the phone with a yawn.

"Yes, this is Chaz."

"Hi, Chaz, it's Sean again. Don't hang up."

She really should've added his number to her address book. Her heart thudded against her rib cage as adrenaline surged. "Sean. What a surprise."

"You know I'm in town. You saw me, just like I saw you."

She inhaled a sharp breath. "Okay then, why are you here? What do you want?"

"I want to meet up. There are things we need to talk about."

"I don't know..."

"You can't hide forever, you know."

She let her eyes drift shut. It was tempting — hiding forever. If she did that, she'd never have to face the truth of what the past held in its grimy little hands. So many secrets, so much unknown. The regret swamped her sometimes, but she'd gotten better at putting it behind her — as if the past was a creature she could shove into a small room and lock the door on.

"I wasn't hiding," she whispered.

"Yes, you were. But the question is, what were you hiding from? From the police, from me, from the past...That's what I'm still not certain about. Maybe it was all of those things. Was it, sis?"

"Why would I hide from the police?" she asked.

He laughed. "Good question. Why would you? Why would you run away and hide?"

"I'll say it again — I'm not hiding. Yes, maybe I wanted to leave that place and start my life afresh because there was nothing left for me there. But I didn't change my name, did I? It couldn't have been too difficult to locate me because here you are."

"That's true, I suppose."

"You were the one who disappeared without a trace," she said, her voice rising.

"Now, now, no need to get upset. Let's meet tomorrow and we can talk all about it."

She didn't want to see him. But if she didn't meet him, he might never leave. Not to mention the fact that her curiosity might never be sated. She wanted to learn the truth — to find out why he'd left her that way and what'd happened between him and their mother before her death. Where was the money Mum had promised to leave Charmaine?

The sooner Sean left Coral Island and let her get on with her life, the better. She didn't want to give up her new flat and her job, the wedding planning work she'd lined up and the friendships, not to mention Watson, to go on the run all over again because of Sean. No, she'd face him finally and get it over with.

"Fine. We can meet tomorrow."

"Great, and don't skip out on me again. I'm getting tired of the chase, little sister."

Nineteen

~

BEA STOOD on the end of the dock with her phone in her hand. She held it up and snapped a photograph of Taya embracing Evie and Penny at the same time. Then Taya came to embrace her, and Bea took a selfie of the two of them, tears stinging her eyes.

"I'm not leaving forever," Taya said with a laugh. "You're being very dramatic. Especially you, Drew."

Andrew pushed his hands into his pockets with a half smile. "You knew I was dramatic when you agreed to go on that first date with me."

"I knew no such thing," she countered before giving him a passionate kiss.

"I know it's not forever," Bea said, wiping her eyes with her sleeve. "But it's definitely the end of an era. We usually catch up as a foursome every week for lunch. And now it'll be a month before we can do that again. I don't know how often we'll get to have our lunches at the inn from now on."

Taya gave a wry smile. "I'm going to miss you too. And I'm sorry I may not be here for your wedding."

"It's absolutely fine. We're keeping everything very low-key. I get it — you're going to be busy in Fiji. So, think of me when you're lounging beside the pool with a cocktail in your hand," Bea said.

As they spoke, the ferry chugged up to the dock, and workers tied it in place before vehicles began exiting via a large ramp. Taya gave hugs all around, then climbed into her car to drive onto the ferry. Andrew said goodbye and hurried away. Bea chatted with Evie and Penny a few minutes before they had to leave. But she remained behind, waiting for her children to disembark.

It didn't take long for Dani and Harry to appear, backpacks on. A man trailed after Dani, his dark curls carefully groomed, his brown beard flecked with grey. Damien, no doubt. He looked like Bea's peer rather than her daughter's. Dani had convinced her to invite him to attend the wedding as her daughter's date, and Bea was determined to remain cordial to the man, even though she hated the influence he was having on Dani's attitude and choices.

She embraced her children, then offered a hand to Damien. "How lovely to meet you. Welcome to Coral Island."

He shook her hand, glancing about the island rather than making eye contact. "It's very pretty here."

She nodded. "There's no place on earth quite like it. Come on—let's get back to the cottage. I've got dinner in the slow cooker."

They drove to the cottage in the old station wagon. Bea was mostly silent while Dani and Harry prattled on about their studies and their lives in Sydney. It was good to have them back on the island.

Bea never felt quite as happy as she did when her children were around, and she couldn't wait to share this special event in her life with them. They seemed so much more grown up than they had when she first divorced their father the previous year. So many things had happened since then, and they'd had to mature in order to deal with their family splitting up, Bea moving away, their father meeting someone new, changes to Dani's degree of choice and Harry's health.

They'd both coped so well with all of it that Bea sometimes wondered if maybe they were hiding their true feelings. Perhaps that was why Dani was dating a man almost twice her age.

"I hope you like beef massaman," Bea said as she pulled into the driveway.

The cottage perched behind the dunes with a view of the beach between a clump of pandanus and sea grasses. The entire vista was bathed in the golden light of afternoon.

"Love it," Harry said.

"I'm vegan," Damien added.

Bea frowned. "Dani, you didn't tell me that."

"Yes, I did."

"Really? I must've forgotten then. I'm sorry. I'm sure I can find something for you to eat, Damien."

"Wonderful," he replied as he stepped out of the car.

Harry and Dani carried their backpacks into the cottage. Damien followed without his, since he was staying at a bed-and-breakfast nearby. Bea had a rule for both of her children — no sleepovers with their girlfriends or boyfriends. It was a rule she'd established as soon as Dani began dating and one she intended to continue until they were both married, much to Dani's dismay.

"It's embarrassing, Mum," she'd said when Bea reminded her of the rule. "Damien is going to think I'm a teenager."

"You were a teenager two years ago, honey. And it doesn't matter—the rule would still apply if you were thirty years old."

Dani and Harry both carried their bags to their bedrooms while Bea dished up dinner in the kitchen. Damien hung about awkwardly, in silence. She tried to engage him in chitchat, but he responded with single-word answers until she gave up. Instead, he preferred to wander around her living room, staring at each picture or piece of art from various angles, tipping his head to one side, then the other, over and over again.

They sat together around the small kitchen table and ate. Bea heated up a bowl of lentil and vegetable soup for Damien that she'd had left over in the fridge from the previous evening. She served it with the sourdough bread she'd baked that morning at the café. The rest of them ate beef massaman with homemade naan bread.

"Did you know that naan bread is Indian and massaman is Thai?" Damien asked as he stirred his soup carefully. "So, it doesn't really go together."

"Wow, that's interesting," Bea said in her best company voice.

Dani shot her a warning look. She'd have to try harder not to sound peeved. Her daughter knew her too well.

After dinner, they all sat around the living room and played a game of Scotland Yard. It'd been one of their favourite family games when the kids were little. Dad came down from his house up on the hill to join them, and the five of them had a lot of fun trying their best to figure out who was the criminal and where on the board they were located.

Each of the others played the part of a detective from Scotland Yard, hot on the case. It took Bea ages to figure out that Harry was the fugitive from justice. He was so good at keeping his piece just out of reach. Damien didn't seem particularly invested in the game and instead wandered off to sit on the porch before they'd finished. When the fugitive was revealed, Dani left to join him.

When Bea went to bed, she was grateful they'd managed to have a peaceful and enjoyable evening together. Her father drove Damien to his accommodations so Bea could rest and prepare herself for the next day, which would be a busy one full of last-minute wedding preparations.

She was applying moisturiser to her face when Aidan called.

"Hello, Rushton," he said.

She laughed. "You won't be able to call me that soon."

"I know—I'm just sneaking it in while I can. Are you sure you want to change your name? You kept your maiden name all these years. You don't have to change it now if you'd rather not."

She loved that he was so concerned about her happiness. "Truthfully, I think I kept it as Rushton because of you. That was your pet name for me, and I couldn't bear to part with it."

"I wish I'd known how you felt." He frowned.

She smiled to herself. "I thought you'd moved on. Besides, I loved him in my own way, and I believed he was the right one for me. So, I'm learning to live with no regrets."

"Wanted you then, now and forevermore," he said, warming her heart. "And I can't wait to call you Mrs Whitlock."

They spoke for a few more minutes, then Bea yawned and Aidan said they should both go to bed and get some rest.

"Will you be able to sleep?" she asked him.

"I don't know. Not very sleepy yet."

"There's no backing out now," she teased.

He hesitated. "Really? Are you sure? Maybe I've changed my mind..."

"Don't you dare!"

He laughed. "I'll see you tomorrow, Rushton."

She hung up the phone and pressed it to her chest for a minute, regarding her own reflection in the bathroom mirror. He was truly the one for her. Even when he was teasing, she couldn't love him more.

* * *

The next day, Bea took Dani and Harry to the formal wear shop to try on their clothes for the wedding. Dani had bought a dress in Sydney, but the tailor at the shop had agreed to adjust it for her. Harry had rented a suit that'd arrived a few days earlier. They both tried on their outfits and walked out to where Bea sat.

Dani looked beautiful in an off-the-shoulder cobalt blue dress with an asymmetrical hemline. She'd match the ocean that encircled the island. Grace had a dress in the same colour but with spaghetti straps and a long skirt. Harry was handsome in his black suit with the open collar.

Bea clapped her hands together. "I can't believe how grown up you look."

Harry sighed. "Mum, we're both adults."

"I know, but I still see you as a five-year-old."

"That's encouraging," Dani quipped. She spun around in place. "What do you think? I tried to pick something you might like."

"I love it," Bea replied, giving Dani a quick hug. "I don't want to wrinkle you, but you look stunning."

While the tailor was taking measurements to adjust Harry's cuffs, Taya called, so Bea stepped outside to answer.

"Hello, stranger. How's it going in Fiji?"

Taya sounded far away. "I'm sitting by the pool with a Mai Thai and I thought of you."

Bea laughed. "I wish I was there with you!"

"I do too."

"Is it amazing?"

"The resort is lovely. There's a lot for me to work on, though. They've got some issues, since it's a new resort. I'm glad I came. It's going to be a big job."

"You'll be great," Bea replied.

"I'm really beginning to regret not coming to your wedding, though."

"It's fine. I already told you that."

"I know, but I don't want to miss it."

"I promise there will be a video and lots of photos."

Taya sighed. "Okay. That will have to do, I suppose."

"How are the staff treating you?"

"They're being very respectful. It's obvious they know about my father. But it does make my job easier, so I'm not complaining. Also, they've put me in the executive suite, which I'm sure they wouldn't do for any other member of staff who visited. It's like I'm on a luxury holiday, but I'm here for work."

"Well, I'm glad you're having a good time."

"I am. I was sad to leave Coral Island and walk away from everyone. I miss Drew already, and I know it won't take me long to feel homesick. I wasn't sure I was ready to do this when I was seated on the ferry, crossing the strait. But now that I'm here, I know I'm ready. I've got the experience, and I feel confident. I'm excited to go forward from here."

"You're more than ready for it, honey. And I'm really proud of you. You're going to smash it."

"Thanks, Bea. You're always the encouraging voice I need to hear."

Twenty

THE DAY after her unexpected phone call with her brother, Charmaine rode her bike to the dock where she'd arranged to meet him. It wasn't far—she could've walked—but she hadn't ridden in days, and she decided to take a loop around town before their meeting so she could work some of the nervous tension from her body.

Finally meeting up with her brother after three years was causing a knot to form in her stomach. After pedalling around town like mad for ten minutes, that knot began to shift, and even though she had sweat dripping down the sides of her face and the small of her back when she made it to the dock, she felt much better in general.

On the way back through town, she spied Penny and Rowan outside a sushi restaurant and stopped her bike, puffing hard, to say hello.

"Back from your honeymoon, Mr and Mrs Clements?" she asked.

Penny rushed down to kiss her cheek. "It's so good to see you. Yes, we had a fabulous time, but it's Hathaway now. We both decided to change our surname given everything that's happened with Rowan's stepdad, and Hathaway was Rowan's name before his mother married Buck."

"Hathaway. I like it — a nice strong name, easy to spell. It's perfect." She wasn't sure what you should say to congratulate a couple on a name change and stumbled over the words. "I'm glad you've had a chance to relax and enjoy yourselves."

Rowan took Penny's hand. "How nice to see you, Chaz. I hope you've recovered from the wedding."

Charmaine grinned. "The storm was certainly challenging. But in the end, we made it all happen, mostly thanks to you."

He shrugged. "It worked out."

"It certainly did," Penny added as she linked her fingers through Rowan's and looked up at him with a glowing smile.

"Was New Zealand nice?"

"It was lovely."

"Although we hardly left the room," Rowan said with a wink.

Penny slapped his arm. "People don't need details, honey."

He laughed. "Just kidding."

Charmaine couldn't help feeling warm all over at the sight of the two of them. They had the kind of love and friendship she longed to find. But given her situation, she doubted it would ever happen for her. She found it so difficult to let anyone get close to her, let alone share a life with her.

"Thank you for everything you did, by the way. I didn't get a chance to say that after the reception since you had to leave. But I really appreciate all your hard work on the wedding. I couldn't have done it without you," Penny said.

"You're very welcome," Charmaine replied. "I enjoyed it. I didn't realise how much fun it would be pulling a wedding together. And then managing things on the day — it was really satisfying to see all our efforts come to fruition."

"You certainly have a gift for keeping everyone calm," Penny replied with a laugh. "There were a few times I thought

I might have to breathe into a brown paper bag, but you got me through it."

Charmaine wasn't used to receiving so much praise, and she shifted from foot to foot uncomfortably, then changed the subject. "Have you seen Sam lately? She hasn't come to the florist shop in a while."

Penny's brow furrowed. "Really? No, I haven't. I've been so busy with the wedding and honeymoon, I haven't thought about her. I wonder how she's doing."

"Usually, she's at the shop every afternoon after school. The term's almost over, but she hasn't been in lately. I'm sure she's busy with end-of-year activities." Charmaine had a tendency to turn everything into a disaster.

It was likely that Sam was perfectly fine and she was making something out of nothing. But she couldn't get out of her head the fight Sam's dad had with Betsy and the things Sam had said when Charmaine last spoke with her. The little girl was caught in the middle of something Charmaine didn't really understand, and she was concerned about her.

"I'm sure she's fine. But I can drop in to her place and check on her, if you like. I drive past it all the time on my way home."

"That would be great. Thank you." Charmaine wasn't usually one to worry about other people's children, but there was something about Sam. She seemed so alone in the world. It reminded Charmaine of herself at that age.

"I've been meaning to talk to Bea about that whole situation with Betsy and Buck and their American names," Penny said. "We should look into that."

"You don't think Betsy was telling the truth?" Charmaine asked.

"I'm sure she was, but it would be interesting to see if there's any evidence of the two of them before the name change. Maybe there'll be some information about their cult."

"I didn't tell anyone this, but she and her son had a huge fight a few weeks ago when I was new to the island. I didn't know much about her at the time, so I didn't know what to make of it. But it was a little concerning."

"Do you know what they were fighting about?"

"Something about her being a liar and a fraud."

"Wow. That's interesting," Penny said, eyes narrowed. "Let's all get together and do some investigating soon."

"Sounds good." Charmaine waved goodbye to Penny and Rowan.

She was now officially running late for her meeting with Sean. She could only hope he'd given up and left the island in a huff. The likelihood of that was slim. With a groan of reluctance, she climbed onto her bike and pedalled in the direction of the dock. There was a shelter at the opening of the dock with bench seats on either side. She stopped there and waited, one hand shielding her eyes.

"Where'd you get the bike?" Sean asked with a smile as he stepped out of the shadows, a black backpack slung over one shoulder.

She set the bike against a wall and went to embrace him. "Sorry. I'm sweaty."

He kissed her cheek. "It's good to see you, sis."

"I still can't believe you're here."

"In the flesh," he said, waving both hands up and down his body as if revealing a magic trick.

"You wanted to talk, so let's talk." The sooner this conversation was over, the sooner she could get back to her life. Seeing Sean again like this stirred up a lot of emotions — he was her brother, she loved him, she'd missed him more than she'd realised.

The expression on his face, the way he spoke to her—she could recall all the good times they'd had as siblings during their tumultuous childhood. The times they'd stuck together, when he'd defended her against bullies or climbed the pantry shelves to get the porridge down that she loved for breakfast. Memories piled up around her like soiled crockery.

He tipped his head to one side. "I'm starved. You hungry?"

She shrugged. "I could eat."

"Where can we go?"

She pointed at the Coral Island Bakery. "They've got sausage rolls, but they're pretty ordinary. Plus, you've got to ring the bell to find anyone."

"That's a no. I'm not big into pastries."

She hadn't wanted to introduce him to her new friends, but there was really nowhere else to recommend at that time of day. "How about Bea's Coffee? It's attached to a great bookshop, and they have amazing baked goods."

"Sounds like a winner."

They walked side by side over the street to the café. She locked her bike to railing, then went inside. She glanced around the café and was glad to see that Bea wasn't there. At least she wouldn't have to answer questions about her brother immediately, although no doubt the news of their meeting would get back to Bea in short order.

A table near the back of the café was free, so they sat across from one another. Charmaine ordered a caramel slice and cappuccino, and Sean opted for a slice of black forest cake and a long black. They made idle chitchat while they waited for the food and coffee, then sat in silence as the waitress placed the items on their table.

After she was gone, Charmaine spoke first. "What are you doing here, Sean?"

He stirred sugar into his coffee. "I wanted to see you."

"Why?"

"There are things we need to discuss."

"Such as?"

167

"Haven't you missed me?"

She rolled her eyes. "Yes, of course I have. But..."

"But what?"

"You know what." She shook her head, slowly savouring a bite of caramel slice.

"Whatever you think I did, you're wrong."

"Mum was going to live—that's what the doctors said. She was supposed to recover."

"But she didn't. It was a stroke. Sometimes people die from them."

"Yes, but you were there. You saw her last. You visited her in the rehabilitation facility."

"So did you."

She took another bite, thinking carefully about what words to use. She didn't want to accuse her brother of anything falsely, but there were so many things that hadn't made sense to her at the time. Now that she was seated in front of him, her words sounded silly, hollow.

"That's true. I did."

"What are you saying, Chaz? You think I had something to do with her death?"

"I spoke to the nurse in charge, and she said you'd been in the room before she died and the two of you had been arguing. Then, a few days later, the accountant called to say that you'd already dealt with the inheritance and there was nothing left. What was I supposed to think?"

"Mum left a will. Did you know that?"

"What? Did she?" Charmaine didn't recall anyone talking about a will.

"If you'd asked more questions, you would've heard I didn't claim the inheritance—I went to their office to get the will but I didn't *take* anything. I'm the executor."

"Really? Is that true?"

"I can't believe you'd think that of me."

She felt foolish then. Perhaps she'd jumped to conclusions about Sean. He'd been a troubled teenager and had given their mother no end of grief for much of his life. But the things she'd suspected him of doing were outlandish when spoken openly in the light of day.

"I've known you a long time," she objected.

"Yes, but I've changed. I thought you could see that."

Maybe he wasn't the boy he'd been — the boy who resorted to violence if he didn't get his way, who would steal money from his mother's purse for himself and his friends to spend on drugs or shoes, whatever took their fancy at the time.

"I can see it," she admitted. "I'm sorry if I misjudged you." He might've been a troubled teen, but it didn't make sense for him to turn against the woman who'd always taken him in and helped him when he needed it, even if they had fought incessantly for years.

"I loved Mum. You know that."

"You and Mum never got along, and I suppose I feared the worst. I guess I know you wouldn't hurt Mum. I didn't really believe it until you disappeared. Then I figured you were running from the police for a reason."

He reached for her hand and squeezed it. "I'm your brother. I would never hurt you or Mum. I didn't disappear— I went away for a while to clear my head. I was grieving, not thinking clearly. Surely you of all people can understand the need to escape."

"You're not on the run?"

He laughed. "No, I'm not on the run. But I do need a place to stay."

"You can stay with me—for a little while, at least. I don't have much room, but the couch is yours, if you'd like it."

"Thanks. I appreciate it. It won't be for long—only a few days. I promise."

"That's fine. It'll be nice to have the company."

"I've got a letter for you from Mum's solicitor." He picked up his backpack from the floor and unzipped it, pulled out a folder containing a sheet of paper and handed it to her.

She read it quickly. It was a letter outlining how she was named as a beneficiary of her mother's will and she should contact the solicitor to find out more. She stared at it in disbelief. All this time, she'd thought the worst of her brother. It seemed she'd been completely wrong about him. She should've stayed in town after the funeral, but she hadn't known about the will or the solicitor. The accountant must've been in the dark as well, since she hadn't said anything about it.

"Thanks, Sean," Charmaine said. "It's hard for me to understand how this all happened. I thought I would've known if Mum had a will or hired a solicitor."

"She told me about it, since I'm the executor," Sean replied.

"I'm glad she included someone in her plans." Charmaine folded her arms across her chest. "She was always so secretive. At least she was with me. If I asked her questions, she'd change the subject or get snippy with me to force me to let it go."

"She was a handful," Sean admitted. "I reacted badly, though. You took it in stride."

"I buried my feelings. Not quite the same thing." She grunted. "But I'm learning to put it behind me and move forward. Sunshine and sand are good remedies."

"I like your way of thinking." Sean grinned. "So, why did you come here? Was it only for the sun and sand, or do you have some other reason for selecting this small tropical island in the middle of nowhere as your new home?"

She drank the last of her cappuccino and set the empty mug back in its saucer. "Do you recall Mum ever mentioning this place? About Coral Island?"

He shook his head, brow furrowed. "No. Do you?"

"She mentioned it once. She was talking about her sister — apparently, our aunt lived here."

"That's interesting," Sean said, stirring his coffee with a spoon. "I do remember she had a sister. Mum talked about her family more when I was younger. You wouldn't remember that, I suppose."

"I was too little. But she spoke about it after her initial stroke, so I couldn't really understand what she was saying. But now that she's gone, I'd like to reconnect with her family. I have no idea why she was estranged from them, but maybe if I find our aunt, I can ask her about it."

"There were a few phone calls with family in those early years. And I vaguely recall Mum travelling to see her parents when I was really small."

"Do you remember where they lived?"

He shook his head. "No, but it was in Queensland because I can picture the flight. It was my first time on a plane. The destination was somewhere in Queensland, but I have no idea exactly where. Wherever it was, it wasn't as built-up or busy as Sydney."

"Why have I never heard about this before now?"

He shrugged. "You never asked."

"Well, I'm asking now. I want to know what Mum said about her family. Let's pay the bill and go back to my flat, and you can tell me everything you know."

Twenty-One

BEATRICE'S WEDDING day dawned sunny and bright. The air was still. Birds dived and chirped as they captured insects and awakened the world with their song. Bea ate scrambled eggs on toast, seated on the back deck with a view of her beach.

She loved it there — her favourite place in the world. But it wouldn't be her home for much longer. She and Aidan had decided she'd move in with him and leave the cottage behind. His house was much bigger and would be perfect for guests when they came to stay. She was excited about the change, but would miss the cottage. Dad had decided to rent it out for a little extra income.

When she went inside, there were boxes stacked all around the walls with her possessions inside. She hadn't finished packing yet—that would have to wait until after the honeymoon. But her essentials had already been transported to Aidan's house, apart from her suitcase and the things she needed for the wedding.

She couldn't wrap her head around the idea that the two of them were finally getting married — would spend the rest of their lives together. She'd often dreamed of this moment at various times in her life. Even when married to Preston, the imagery of her ending up with Aidan had haunted her sleeping hours.

She was grateful her reality had mirrored the happiest dream, and that dream had really only just begun. Aidan's daughter lived with her mother most of the year, and Bea's kids were in Sydney. That meant the two of them had empty nests the majority of the time and could travel, go out to dinner, snorkel or do whatever it was they wanted to do whenever Aidan wasn't working at the primary school.

She'd hired Candice Gossamer to manage the café and planned to let her handle the business during school holidays so she and Aidan could go globetrotting. Candace had waited tables for a while and was taking a year off between high school and university, so she was the perfect choice. And already, Bea was grateful for her efficiency and work ethic.

In the kitchen, Dani and Harry were busily cooking breakfast. Dani's blonde hair was caught up in a messy bun, and she wore a long T-shirt as her PJs. Harry was in a pair of cotton shorts. His brown curls had been shorn into a more manageable length, just below his ears, as a wedding gift to Bea, although she had assured him she liked his long hair and the only thing she wanted as a gift was for him to be healthy and well. He'd improved so much since his bout of Lyme disease that he seemed like a different person. He was joking and laughing with his sister as he stirred a pan of scrambled eggs and bacon.

"Did you enjoy your eggs? Because there's plenty more if you're hungry," Harry said when Bea stepped up to the stove to peer around his shoulder.

"I've had enough, thanks. It was delicious, but my stomach is feeling a little strange this morning."

"Not nervous, I hope," Dani said with a wink as she slathered butter over pieces of sourdough toast.

"I am a little."

"You know you don't have to go through with it, Mum," she said. "There's no rule that you have to marry someone." She grabbed a piece of bacon from where it was draining on the paper towel beside the frying pan and took a bite.

Harry slapped at her hand. "Hey, stop it. Wait for me to dish up."

"I'm not following any rules," Bea replied as she poured coffee into her favourite mug.

"Damien says the reason you're remarrying so quickly is because your generation believes there's a societal requirement that you must date for a certain period of time, and then get married. That you can't simply live and let live, or choose an alternative lifestyle the way he does."

Bea bit down on her lip to keep from replying with the retort that leapt to mind. "Interesting..."

"He's right, though. You don't have to get married. Look at Aunty Taya — she and Andrew are dating, they care about each other, but she's out there living her life, building her career. She's amazing. She's forging her own path, creating her own destiny. That's what Damien says we all should do."

Bea pushed a smile over her lips. "She *is* amazing—you're right. But she's already been married and raised a child, so she's not exactly shunning those things. And I'm choosing to do what I *want* to do by marrying Aidan. I'm not doing it because of some silly rule but because we're in love, and I'm not having second thoughts." The irritation that burned in her gut quickly replaced the nerves she was feeling.

There was no point picking a fight. It was her wedding day, and Dani was her maid of honour. She didn't need them to be angry with one another as they walked down the aisle. She wanted harmony and peace. It was going to be a good day.

One of the very best of her life and Damien's opinion meant nothing to her.

* * *

The morning passed quickly. After breakfast, Dani and Bea joined Penny and Evie at the hairdressing salon, where they all got their hair and makeup done. They sipped champagne and ate chocolate. They talked and laughed together over what was ahead. Bea's anxiety was gone, and in its place was a building excitement. This day had been a long time in coming, and now that it was here, she would savour every single moment of it.

When she got to the Blue Shoal Inn, her father was waiting for her in the room she'd booked. He looked so handsome in his black suit with the white shirt open at the collar. His grey hair was stylishly smoothed back, and his blue eyes sparkled at the sight of her.

"You look beautiful, Beatrice," he said, kissing her cheek.

"Thanks, Dad," she replied, giving him a warm hug. "I'm so glad you're here with me."

"Nowhere else I'd rather be."

Dani joined her in the room while Harry went looking for Aidan. Before long, there was a knock at the door, and Aidan's daughter, Grace, joined them. She'd cut her hair into a short bob, but was otherwise the same gangly teen girl who'd showed up unannounced the previous year and blown their lives apart. But Bea wouldn't change a thing about what'd happened since in the end, it had only brought her and Aidan closer together, and now he had a wonderful daughter to add joy to his life.

She embraced Grace with a smile. "You're here — now the party is complete. And you look lovely."

"Thank you," Grace said softly. "You do too."

When the music began downstairs, Bea's heart skittered in

her chest. It was time to get started. She looped her arm through her father's and followed Dani and Grace down the inn's winding staircase. At the bottom of the stairs, she waited for the girls to walk the short pathway outside to the rose garden, then started off after them. The alcove was sheltered by an archway and fence covered with climbing roses. Beyond the fence were rows of white seats containing the few guests they'd invited to witness their nuptials.

Bea's heart was in her throat. She choked back tears as she walked. The music was emotive, bringing to the surface all the things she felt — content, fulfilled, excited and more. Dad patted her arm and offered her a loving glance. A photographer snapped photos of them together. And then she was beneath the archway and walking up the aisle.

The look on Aidan's face made her breath catch. He beamed at her, then took her hand in his and held it tenderly.

She didn't recall the vows she made during her first wedding. She'd been so nervous, she could barely get the words out. But this time, she fixed her attention on everything that was said, every glance from her groom, every laugh or sigh from the guests. It was all so precious to her this time around, and she didn't want to forget a single moment.

When the ceremony was over, she was giddy with happiness.

Aidan kissed her, then dipped her in front of the audience, to their great delight. She laughed as he righted her again and whispered in her ear, "I love you, Mrs Whitlock."

"Back at you, Mr Whitlock," she replied.

The reception was inside, so they all made their way gradually from the rose garden into the inn as the sun set beyond the trees behind the tiny hamlet. Aidan took Bea's hand for their first dance, and she thought she might faint from the romance of the moment. It was everything she'd hoped for and more.

She couldn't imagine life could be happier than it was that day.

* * *

When the bride and groom had finished their first dance Penny danced with her new husband.

"It feels like this was us only yesterday," she whispered in Rowan's ear.

"I know what you mean."

"Who would've thought all those years ago that you and I would be married and that Bea and Aidan would be too?"

"Not me," Rowan admitted. "Although, I would've liked the idea."

She laughed. "Life has taken some twists and turns, but I'm pretty happy with how things have ended up."

"And this isn't the end," he said, one eyebrow arched as he spun her twirling across the dance floor.

She threw her head back to laugh at the ceiling just as she spied Taya in the corner. Taya waved, and she let go of Rowan's hand to run over and greet her friend.

"You made it! I didn't think you were coming."

"I wasn't," Taya said. "But I couldn't stand thinking of you all having fun without me."

Penny gave Taya a big hug and took her hands. "I'm glad. We missed you. Come and see Evie. She'll be so happy you're here."

Evie was seated beside Charmaine. The two of them were deep in conversation, huddled around a mobile phone.

"Look who's here," Penny said.

Evie squealed and threw her arms around Taya while jumping in place. "I knew it! I knew you wouldn't miss the whole thing."

When Taya had given the bride and groom a hug, she

returned to their table. She smoothed her hair back into its usual perfect style. "What were you two so engrossed with when we walked over here before?'

Evie exchanged a glance with Charmaine. "It can wait. We're here to enjoy a wedding, not to obsess over Buck and Betsy."

Penny peered over Charmaine's shoulder, but couldn't see the phone screen. "What's going on?"

Evie cleared her throat. "We were just sitting here..."

"Not dancing, of course, since we're both single," Charmaine added.

"Clearly..." Evie agreed with a nod. "And we started talking about Betsy and that revelation she made about Buck changing his name, and her changing hers, because of a cult. So, we thought we'd see if we could find anything out about the cult. We've all been too busy to look into it, but I've been so curious."

Penny sat beside Charmaine and leaned forwards. "And did you find anything?"

"We did."

Charmaine sighed. "I don't really want to get involved. Betsy's my boss, and I consider her a friend as well."

"You don't have to say anything," Evie replied, patting Charmaine's arm. "I'll do all the talking. So, we discovered that when we put Buck's old name, Samuel Jay Gilmore, into the search engine, we don't really get anything at all. He changed his name a long time ago, before the internet was a thing. But what's interesting is that there's a Betsy Anne Gilmore who's wanted by police in California."

"What? I thought Betsy was from Indiana. That's what she always says." Penny frowned.

"I know, but Buck's driver's licence is from California. What I don't know is if this is the same woman. But we were reading up about it because the coincidence is certainly interesting. About fifty years ago, Betsy Anne Gilmore-Alton kidnapped her son when she was in the middle of a custody dispute with the boy's father and fled the state. It says here that authorities never discovered her whereabouts, and she is still wanted in the state of California. Gilmore is her maiden name, and when she married Francis Alton, she hyphenated her surname."

"Wow," Penny replied. "But it might not be her, right?"

"Right. We don't know for sure. It could be a coincidence that there's a woman with the same last name as Samuel and lives in the same state as his driver's licence was issued, who's wanted and who also has a son who's the same age as the boy who was abducted."

"But she didn't really abduct him. She's his mother."

"True. It's complicated, I suppose. But his father was fighting for partial custody when she took the boy and he's spent the past fifty or so years searching for his son," Charmaine said.

Taya shook her head slowly from side to side. "This is possibly a wild goose chase, but if it's the Betsy we know, it makes a lot more sense that she'd change her name and move to a remote island off the coast of Australia in order to hide her son from a custody dispute than to leave a cult behind."

"I don't know much about cults," Penny added, "but I think you're right."

"Oh, wait. There's a photo," Evie said, flicking through images on her phone before holding it up for the rest of them to see.

Penny squinted at the image. It was an old photograph of a woman with her hair curled around her face. She smiled at the camera in a confident, yet nonchalant way.

"That could be Betsy," Taya said. "She has all those photographs of herself as a dancer hung up around the florist shop."

"That's true," Charmaine replied, taking a closer look. "It certainly looks like her."

Evie didn't say anything, but her face paled.

"What's wrong?" Penny asked, her brow furrowed.

Evie held the phone closer to her face and studied the image. "I could be wrong, but this woman looks so familiar to me."

"She looks familiar to all of us," Penny agreed. "I'm sure that's Betsy. If we can get into the shop and compare the photo to the ones on her walls, I bet we'll find they match."

"Maybe," Taya said slowly. "I don't know."

"I know where I've seen her face before," Evie exclaimed suddenly, her face brightening.

"Where?" Taya asked.

"In the photos..."

"I know. We were just talking about that," Penny replied, wondering if Evie had been paying attention to anything they'd said.

"No, I mean the old photos — the ones I developed for Bea. She's the mystery woman from the photos Bea found in the wall of the beach cottage."

Goose bumps travelled up Penny's arms and over the back of her skull. "You're right." She reached for the phone and scrolled, looking for more. She found a photograph of a little boy. He had dark hair in a bowl cut and grinned at the camera, his eyes squinting.

"And this is the little boy who was standing beside her in the photos. This could be the man we know as Frank Norton. This is Samantha's father," Penny said. "He looks just like Sam."

* * *

Continue the series...

Ready to read book 5 in the *Coral Island* series so you can keep following Penny, Charmaine and the rest of the Coral Island crew? Find out the truth about Betsy and Buck. Buy the next book in this series!

Want to know about all of my new releases? You can get on my VIP reader list by subscribing via my website, and you'll also get a free book.

Also by Lilly Mirren

WOMEN'S FICTION

CORAL ISLAND SERIES

The Island

After twenty five years of marriage and decades caring for her two children, on the evening of their vow renewal, her husband shocks her with the news that he's leaving her.

The Beach Cottage

Beatrice is speechless. It's something she never expected — a secret daughter. She and Aidan have only just renewed their romance, after decades apart, and he never mentioned a child. Did he know she existed?

The Blue Shoal Inn

Taya's inn is in trouble. Her father has built a fancy new resort in Blue Shoal and hired a handsome stranger to manage it. When the stranger offers to buy her inn and merge it with

183

the resort, she wants to hate him but when he rescues a stray dog her feelings for him change.

Island Weddings

Charmaine moves to Coral Island and lands a job working at a local florist shop. It seems as though the entire island has caught wedding fever, with weddings planned every weekend. It's a good opportunity for her to get to know the locals, but what she doesn't expect is to be thrown into the middle of a family drama.

The Island Bookshop

Evie's book club friends are the people in the world she relies on most. But when one of the newer members finds herself confronted with her past, the rest of the club will do what they can to help, endangering the existence of the bookshop without realising it.

An Island Reunion

It's been thirty five years since the friends graduated from Coral Island State Primary School and the class is returning to the island to celebrate. A reunion can mean only one thing — Coral Island's secrets and lies will finally unravel and the truth will be revealed.

THE WARATAH INN SERIES

The Waratah Inn

Wrested back to Cabarita Beach by her grandmother's sudden death, Kate Summer discovers a mystery buried in the past that changes everything.

One Summer in Italy

Reeda leaves the Waratah Inn and returns to Sydney, her

husband, and her thriving interior design business, only to find her marriage in tatters. She's lost sight of what she wants in life and can't recognise the person she's become.

The Summer Sisters

Set against the golden sands and crystal clear waters of Cabarita Beach three sisters inherit an inn and discover a mystery about their grandmother's past that changes everything they thought they knew about their family...

Christmas at The Waratah Inn

Liz Cranwell is divorced and alone at Christmas. When her friends convince her to holiday at The Waratah Inn, she's dreading her first Christmas on her own. Instead she discovers that strangers can be the balm to heal the wounds of a lonely heart in this heartwarming Christmas story.

EMERALD COVE SERIES

Cottage on Oceanview Lane

When a renowned book editor returns to her roots, she rediscovers her strength & her passion in this heartwarming novel.

Seaside Manor Bed & Breakfast

The Seaside Manor Bed and Breakfast has been an institution in Emerald Cove for as long as anyone can remember. But things are changing and Diana is nervous about what the future might hold for her and her husband, not to mention the historic business.

Bungalow on Pelican Way

Moving to the Cove gave Rebecca De Vries a place to hide from her abusive ex. Now that he's in jail, she can get back to living her life as a police officer in her adopted hometown working alongside her intractable but very attractive boss, Franklin.

Chalet on Cliffside Drive

At forty-four years of age, Ben Silver thought he'd never find love. When he moves to Emerald Cove, he does it to support his birth mother, Diana, after her husband's sudden death. But then he meets Vicky.

Christmas in Emerald Cove

The Flannigan family has been through a lot together. They've grown and changed over the years and now have a blended and extended family that doesn't always see eye to eye. But this Christmas they'll learn that love can overcome all of the pain and differences of the past in this inspiring Christmas tale.

HOME SWEET HOME SERIES

Home Sweet Home

Trina is starting over after a painful separation from her husband of almost twenty years. Grief and loss force her to return to her hometown where she has to deal with all of the things she left behind to rebuild her life, piece by piece; a hometown she hasn't visited since high school graduation.

No Place Like Home

Lisa never thought she'd leave her high-profile finance job in the city to work in a small-town bakery. She also never expected to still be single in her forties.

HISTORICAL FICTION

Beyond the Crushing Waves

An emotional standalone historical saga. Two children plucked from poverty & forcibly deported from the UK to Australia. Inspired by true events. An unforgettable tale of loss, love, redemption & new beginnings.

Under a Sunburnt Sky

Inspired by a true story. Jan Kostanski is a normal Catholic boy in Warsaw when the nazis invade. He's separated from his neighbours, a Jewish family who he considers kin, by the ghetto wall. Jan and his mother decide that they will do whatever it takes to save their Jewish friends from certain death. The unforgettable tale of an everyday family's fight against evil, and the unbreakable bonds of their love.

MYSTERIES

White Picket Lies

Fighting the demons of her past Toni finds herself in the midst of a second marriage breakdown at forty seven years of age. She struggles to keep depression at bay while doing her best to raise a wayward teenaged son and uncover the identity of the killer.

In this small town investigation, it's only a matter of time until friends and neighbours turn on each other.

Cast of Characters

As the *Coral Island* series grows, the cast of characters does too. I hope this handy reference will help you keep them sorted!

* * *

Aidan Whitlock - former professional footballer, current primary school PE teacher.

Andrew Reddy - The new manager at *Paradise Resort.*

Annie Draper - Bea's friend from Sydney.

Beatrice Rushton - previously married and living in Sydney, now a resident of Coral Island.

Betsy Norton - Elderly, American, owns the florist shop.

Bradford Rushton - Bea's younger brother, owns a charter fishing company out of Airlie Beach.

Brett O'Hanley - Beatrice & Aidan's contractor.

Buck Clements - Rowan's step father and June's ex-husband.

Camden Futcher - Taya's adult daughter, training to become a chef in Cairns.

Cameron Eldridge - Taya's father and owner of *Paradise Resorts*.

Charmaine Billings - new resident of Coral Island, works at Betsy's Florals.

Damien Lachey - Dani's boyfriend, the professor and architect.

Danita Pike - Bea's adult daughter, lives in Sydney.

Elias Rushton - Bea's father, lives on Coral Island.

Eveleigh (Evie) Mair - Owner of *Eveleigh's Books*, the book shop attached the *Bea's Coffee*.

Finn - Watson, the cat's, official owner.

Frank Norton - Betsy's adult son and Samantha's father.

Fudge - Beatrice's pug.

Grace Allen - Aidan's teenaged daughter.

Harry Pike - Bea's adult son, lives in Sydney.

Henry St James - Penny's stepfather, married to Ruby St James.

Jacqui St James - Rob St James' estranged wife.

Julian St James - Rob's young son.

June Clements - proprietor of the *Coral Cafe* & Rowan's mother.

Kelly Allen - Grace's mother & Aidan's ex-girlfriend.

Luella Rushton - Bea's mother, deceased.

Mary Brown - Penny's grandmother, murder victim.

Ms Gossamer - librarian in Kellyville.

Penny St James - Owner of the *Coral Island Wildlife Rescue Centre*.

Preston Pike - Bea's ex-husband, lives between Sydney & Melbourne.

Robert St James - Penny's brother, travels around to work in construction.

Rowan Clements - June Clements' son, journalist.

Ruby St James - Penny's mother.

Samantha Norton - Betsy's granddaughter & Frank's daughter.

Samuel Jay Gilmore - the name on Buck's California driver's license.

Sean Billings - Charmaine's brother.

Taya Eldridge - Owns the Blue Shoal Inn, is Cameron & Tina Eldridge's daughter.

Tina Eldridge - Taya's mother, married to Cameron.

Todd Futcher - Taya's former husband, deceased.

Watson - Charmaine's visiting cat.

About the Author

Lilly Mirren is an Amazon top 20, Audible top 15 and USA Today Bestselling author who has sold over one million copies of her books worldwide. She lives in Brisbane, Australia with her husband and three children.

She always dreamed of being a writer and is now living that dream. Her books combine heartwarming storylines with realistic characters readers can't get enough of.

Her debut series, The Waratah Inn, set in the delightful Cabarita Beach, hit the *USA Today* Bestseller list and since then, has touched the hearts of hundreds of thousands of readers across the globe.

Made in the USA
Columbia, SC
10 July 2023

20237135R00119